The Prisoner
and other tales of faith

SOLOMON ALTER HALPERN

The Prisoner
and other tales of faith

FELDHEIM PUBLISHERS
Jerusalem / New York
5741 / 1981

Originally published 1968
as Tales of Faith
Second, revised edition, 1972
Reprinted 1975

Hardcover edition: ISBN 0-87306-205-1
Paperback edition: ISBN 0-87306-243-4

Philipp Feldheim Inc.
96 East Broadway
New York, NY 10002

Feldheim Publishers Ltd
POB 6525 / Jerusalem, Israel

Printed in Israel

TABLE OF CONTENTS

INDEX

FOREWORD

The stories in this book were written over the ten years from '52 onwards. Most of them were first published in the youth magazine "Haderech" by Keren Hatorah, London. (The exceptions are "Strange Encounter" and "Test Case", which appeared in "Yeshurun").

Like other collected short-stories they should be read one by one at intervals rather than consecutively, for the stories vary in their style and even in their interpretation of the same event. Many of the stories were written for reading at specific times, for "Haderech" appears at 6 focal points of the Jewish Year. It will also be seen that many stories aim to stress some moral principle of special relevance to our times. To help readers, particularly those wishing to read in classes or groups, in finding stories relevant to times of the year, particular principles, or persons and events in Scripture and later history, I have prepared an index (p. 7).

Serious readers are also advised to use the appendix, to enable them to follow up my sources, if any. Those wishing to know why I take the stories so seriously should read "On Jewish Stories" (p. 11 — but take courage: it contains enough anecdote and polemic to save it from utter boredom). For I have taken the stories seriously enough to engage in considerable research and thought so as to put in as many data and ideas, keep the language as simple and make the plot as interesting as I could manage. I do not of course think that my interpretations are the only correct ones — I shall be happy if all of them are at least possible ones — but I must dissociate myself from those who, intentionally or from lack of learning, produce printed matter which I could not, as a Rabbi, call Jewish or, as a writer, call a story.

Having said all this, let me finish with the hope that Jewish children will find in this book many hours of enjoyment, and may it encourage them to seek in our Torah literature the treasures of which these are but samples.

London, Adar 5727,

Salomon Alter Halpern

ON JEWISH STORIES

The reader will see that in the appendix to this book I have tried to give the sources for my stories (or to make it clear if they are invented). This may seem unnecessary to the more learned of my readers who have met the same stories before in the first sources or at least have heard them told as coming from those sources. However, I think there is great need for writing, and using, that appendix. For one thing, this makes it possible to check how far I have departed from the originals — for it is impossible to re-tell or even to translate a story without giving it one's own interpretation and adding or missing out some details in the process; this may happen quite unintentionally.

There is another point which is important too — to show clearly which stories are pure fiction; for whilst many people will recognize any story in this book which comes from Talmud or Midrash, there are very few indeed who will be able to say: "Now this story certainly did not happen" or "This story is certainly not in any classical source."

Some surprising examples have come my way, and I think it useful to describe them. More than once I have been asked by visitors from Israel, amongst them learned young men, if it was really true that the breastshield from the Temple was in the British Museum. Now I happen to know how they got this idea, and it is a story in itself. About 15 years ago there appeared in youth publications in England and U.S.A., and at some time also in Israel, versions of a story of the stones of the *Choshen Mishpat* being stolen from the British Museum, and recovered with the help of . . . the Maharal of Prague! If I remember it correctly, it was not just the Maharal appearing to someone in a dream, but the Maharal himself in the flesh skipping the centuries, and at the end skipping back to his own time to attend a meeting with his *gabboim*! I remember being rather disgusted with that bit at least, for whilst we find great Zaddikim being granted *kefizath haderech* (miraculous overcoming of distance), I can find no case of, or reason for, leaping back and forth in time.

Curiously enough, at that time the American publication ("Talks & Tales") complained that the English one ("Haderech") had copied its story without permission. In fact the Haderech version was based on a story which appeared in a Yiddish newspaper before the war, in Poland, and presumably the other versions came from there too. Finally however I was told, and verified for myself, that the main plot of the story (without the Maharal etc.) had been written by Sir Arthur Conan Doyle (famous for his Sherlock Holmes stories) in a story entitled "The Jews' Breastplate", in the collection "Round the Fire Stories", 1908. The first Yiddish version was "Der Maharal miPrag mit dem Choshen Mishpot fun Kohen Godol", by R. Yudel Rosenberg, 1913. It seems clear that the Jewish writer extended the plot of the English story. Though I should hesitate to write a complete fiction about a real person myself, I do not blame him for it, because he probably thought it was perfectly obvious to anyone that it was fiction (and if you say: "Listen to this lie: . . ." you are not lying, because you are not deceiving anyone into thinking it truth). In these days, with so much fiction printed, it is quite possible to say that anyone who takes fiction to be fact has only himself to blame. — Nevertheless I prefer to make it clear what is fiction, because a Jewish story, by which I mean more particularly a story with a Torah message or illustrating some Torah point, is often told in a classroom, a youth group or at a family table together with *Divrei Torah;* this makes it more likely for a listener to believe it as truth — or to think, poor child, that he ought to try to believe it, unbelievable though it sounds . . .

That is how those Israelis came to look for the Breastshield in the Museum. Two stories of mine have made at least some people have doubts that they might be true: after "Hidden Treasure" appeared, a Rabbi wrote that his children would give him no peace until he established if there really was a find of Torah records in Cornwall, and after "Strange Encounter" some young people who knew that I had been to Jerusalem (but not Be'er Sheva!) that year asked me if the story (written in the first person) had happened to me. In both cases I had expected everyone to see them clearly as fiction, i.e. something plausible enough at a first reading, something that might indeed have happened, but on consideration quite clearly something planned as a story, with such symmetry and rounding-off as one does not expect in real life, with the reasons for writing it, and writing it in just that way, quite obvious — and more such points.

Plausibility is indeed one of the points necessary to make a story good fiction: a man (who never existed but sounds as if he did) being eaten by a lion in the jungle — that may be good fiction. A man who did or did not exist being eaten by a cow, or for that matter by an elephant, a giraffe or even a hippopotamus (all three, if my memory is any good, confirmed vegetarians) — that is not fiction but merely nonsense. It may of course be told as nonsense, in which case it also does not need to have a moral, — or as a miracle, in which case it must indeed have a moral, (and in fact must either be true or else made clear to be a parable, so that it cannot be called fiction at all).

Unfortunately quite a number of stories which offend against all such rules get printed, because editors cannot find anything better and think that they must print something, and because volunteer writers think that something which is not paid for does not have to be quality, or that stories do not need the same exactness as *Dinim,* or because the particular volunteer is not capable or conscientious enough to verify even his *Dinim.* So, inadvertently and often from the best motives, truth can be turned into falsehood without the excuse of fiction — or any excuse.

Consider the writer who told of the HIDA being given a paper by his teacher the Or Ha-chayim to take from his native Poland to the Kothel Ma'aravi . . . If the writer had cared to look up the HIDA's own sefer *Shem Ha-gedolim* he would have found that HIDA was born in Jerusalem, travelled in many countries but not in Poland, was a pupil (aged 16) of the Or Ha-chayim only when the latter came to Jerusalem in the last year of his life, most of which was lived in Saleh, Morocco! Yet the story was not just dreamed up by that writer; it is told in *Ta'amei Haminhagim* (p. 270, Jerus. '57 edition) as a tradition, but about the Or Ha-chayim and an unnamed follower of his, and apparently taking place in Jerusalem — not in Poland, probably not with HIDA!

Consider the writer who told (in "Haderech") of a first-born donkey, mentioning that it must be given to a Cohen, when a look into his Mishnayoth would have shown him that it must not be given to a Cohen but must be redeemed. Or the writer (in "Sichoth Lanoar" No. 11, probably translated from "Talks & Tales") who thought that the Red Heifer was "sacrificed and burnt on the Altar," when his Chumash should have shown him that it was taken "outside the camp" (in Jerusalem it was taken outside the town); he also thought that the person sprinkling the water becomes impure, when a look into Rashi on the *posuk* (or of course the Talmud) would have shown him that this is not true.

I cannot imagine how the last-named writers excuse their indifference to facts of the Torah, or what they wish to teach Jewish children if they themselves cannot or will not verify their facts.

Mistakes arise somctimes from a mistaken loyalty; the writer remembers something which he heard (or thinks he heard) in his childhood, and does not check up because of course his teacher would not have said anything untrue... Like the Yeshivah boy who insisted that it was the ARI who was the "Chossid called Rabbi Yitzchak" in the story of the Ethrog and Lulav quoted in TaZ (Orach Chayim 651/14) he was sure that his teacher had said so. Maybe he did, but if so he was mistaken, for the episode is told by R. Menachem Rekanti, who lived in the time of Rashba 250 years or so before the ARI.

As for stories written by unorthodox Jews — I cannot consider them Jewish stories for our purpose any more than "kosher-type" food is kosher. They may well contain "messages" which are anti-Torah; but even those that are written so as not to offend anybody, i.e. with no message at all, are by this very harmlessness harmful enough, for what they tell the innocent reader is that Judaism has nothing to say about anything — and that is the wickedest lie of them all.

It is important to state here that in my opinion the message matters most of all, for story-telling with a message is a form of *drush* and *aggadah,* and only fools suppose that in that field "anything can be said." The only difference is that falsehoods in *aggadah* are a little harder to prove, but they are falsehoods just the same — and they are likely to be connected with basic faults in the writer. A writer who puts Torah or any point of it in a bad light is probably trying to "liberate" himself and his readers from Judaism; a writer who presents as a Jewish idea what is in fact opposed by the Torah * is not, for our purpose, a Jewish writer.

Let no one say "Why all this fuss — they are only stories; they are only for children," for psychology shows that childhood impressions and ideas infiltrated during the uncritical receptive state of mind induced by a gripping story have a profound and lasting influence: I am sure that an expert on literature could analyse the debates of any group of people, or even the genesis of major movements, and show which novel implanted which attitude!

This puts a responsibility on parents and teachers regarding the reading (and other entertainment), they promote. It also puts a responsibility on all who are able in one way or other to provide more truly Jewish books with entertainment value. Whilst it is difficult to get an established fiction writer to study Jewish sources to the point of becoming an authority (though he might team up with one), it is worthwhile, in my opinion, for Torah scholars to try to develop a talent for writing, not great or bestselling but at least readable, stories.

Let that be my apology for syphoning off some hundreds of perfectly good hours of a talmudist's time for writing these stories.

* This happens particularly to those who are unable or unwilling to study Torah sources in the original and either read up on Judaism in the writings of anti-Torah men of Jewish or non-Jewish persuasion — such as most encyclopaedias, even if labelled Jewish — or, like the famous writer on 'Chinese Metaphysics" who read up on "China" and "Metaphysics" and combined the information, fabricate a synthetic "Judaism" by a similar process.

THE PRISONER

THE THRONE ROOM was full of courtiers and local dignitaries. King Nimrod, master of all the settled lands, was paying his yearly visit to his southern capital of Ur, and to the temple of Nannar the moon god, whose High Priestess was the king's own daughter.

The room was splendidly decorated. The pillars were sheathed with gold, inlaid with rare stones; the walls were covered with paintings: the king at the head of his army, the king sitting in judgment and, over and over again, the king hunting various kinds of wild animals. For Nimrod prided himself on being the mighty hunter, and indeed life had become much easier for the farmers during his reign because he had killed the wild beasts that used to invade the settled lands. In some districts lions had become rare indeed.

A hush fell on the room. Preceded by standard-bearers, surrounded by guards, and followed by the High Priestess and many priests, soothsayers and advisers, the king made his entry. Everyone bowed low.

When the local governor and various delegations had paid him their homage and spoken formal greetings, a herald proclaimed: "Who seeks Justice? Who is oppressed? Let him step forward and appeal to the most just and illustrious king!"

After a moment's silence, a temple dignitary stepped forward. "May it please your Majesty!" he began. "We have a case of blasphemy and sacrilege. The case is of the greatest importance and involves all the gods, and we beseech Your

Majesty to hear it." The king nodded his assent, and a group of people were led in by temple guards.

"Who is the accuser?" demanded the king. An elderly man stepped forward, and bowed: "I, Your Majesty, Terach son of Nachor, a sculptor and licensed maker of statues of the high gods."

"And who is the accused?"

Two guards led forward a boy of fourteen. His wrists were bound, and he wore prisoner's garb; but from his large dark eyes flashed such earnestness and purpose, so fearlessly did he carry his head, and such calm and resolution were expressed in the handsome young face framed in black locks, that exclamations of admiration escaped some of the onlookers.

"Your Majesty," said the prisoner, "my name is Abram, son of Terach."

The king looked at the father: "You are accusing your own son of a capital crime? And one so young? What kind of jest is this? Can you not keep your child in order yourself?"

"Your Majesty," replied the maker of idols, "how happy would I be if I did not have to bring him to judgment. for I love my son. But he did indeed commit serious crimes, not once but many times, and the punishments I gave him had no effect. He does not fear beatings or being locked up. The only thing that has any effect on him is speaking to him of his duty, but on this matter he gives such answers that I myself become confused about what is right. That is why I pray your Majesty for Justice, not punishment. If he is found innocent, I should be most happy."

The king studied the boy's face for a while, then spoke to the father: "Proceed with your charges!"

"Your Majesty," said Terach, "on many occasions this boy has spoken disrespectfully of the great gods, doubting their power and their very existence. On some occasions he has spoken to worshippers in my private chapel, and even in the temple, declaring that their sacrifices were wasted, that — may I be forgiven for repeating it — the great gods had no power to help or harm. Each time I asked the hearers not to take him seriously, and gave him his punishment myself. But the last thing he did was so serious that I had to inform the priests.

"One day about a month ago I left him in the workshop, as I had business in the market, telling him to take care that no one should touch the holy statues. When I returned, all the statues lay in pieces except the one of Nannar; in front of him was a bowl of food-offerings, and next to him a heavy stick. When I asked the boy what had happened, he said that a woman had brought the offerings, that the gods had quarrelled over them, and that finally Nannar had smashed the others.

"Now I am not a learned priest, but I have never heard of a statue moving; and neither had the priests whom I asked. The boy must have broken the statues himself, and made up the story as a blasphemous jest."

The king turned to Abram: "Is this true?"

"It is, Your Majesty," answered Abram. "I did break the statues."

"Why did you do it?" demanded the king.

"Because I wanted to force my father to admit that the gods cannot move. If they cannot move to defend themselves, how much less can they do good or evil to men?"

There were angry exclamations from the bystanders, but the king commanded silence. He considered for a moment, then he said: "Did you not know that you were doing wrong? In our free country everyone is allowed to choose the god he wishes to worship, but he must not interfere with the worship of others; if he does, he will be punished by the gods and by me, for I am their governor on earth. Which god do you worship then; is it Bel?"

"Your Majesty," answered the prisoner, "neither Bel nor any of the others have any power. There is only one true God, who is the master of the sun, of the moon, and of everything, and He is our true master too."

"Who is that God of whom you speak? Have you seen him? Or who was it that spoke to you of Him?"

"I have not seen the true God, your Majesty," replied Abram. "Neither has He spoken to me. I do not know His name, so I call him 'Lord.' No one told me of Him, yet I know that He exists."

He had spoken so firmly and fearlessly that everybody had forgotten that here was a prisoner on trial for his life; and only a boy, too; they listened to him seriously, and were trying to think of arguments to convince him.

The king spoke again: "If you have not seen Him, nor heard of Him, how else do you profess to know about Him?"

"When I was still a small child," began Abram, "perhaps three or four years old, I began to feel that there must be someone, someone very mighty and good, from whom I receive my life and everything else . . ."

"Yes," interrupted the king, "that was a truly religious feeling. You might become a priest yet. Go on."

"My nurse," continued the boy, "told me stories of the gods; but I could not feel that any of them was the power I felt was there. They sounded like men; jealous of each other, fighting each other . . ."

"Don't worry about that!" said the king. "A priest will explain those mysteries to you — if you are worthy of instruction."

"Then," went on Abram, "when I came out of the darkness . . ."

"What do you mean by that?" interrupted Nimrod.

"Out of the dungeon, your Majesty," said the prisoner. "Until about two years ago I lived in a dark cellar under my father's house."

"What is this?" demanded the king of Terach. "Why did you keep the child in the cellar?"

Terach had grown deathly pale; now he threw himself down before the king.

"Stand up and answer!" thundered Nimrod. "What are you concealing from your king?"

With difficulty, Terach obeyed: "Your Majesty, my life is at your mercy, for I am guilty of a great crime. When this boy was born the soothsayers said he would grow up to defy the King. I was ordered in your Majesty's name to hand him over to be killed. I was weak. In my love for my child I paid no heed to the warning, nor to my king's command. I concealed the child. In his place I surrendered a slave's baby which had just died. Woe is me to have saved the life of a blasphemer!"

After a moment the king replied sternly: "Your crime is great, but I will not pronounce judgment yet. This is no ordinary case; perhaps the gods have made it happen for their greater glory. If that is accomplished your life might be spared." Then turning to Abram he said more kindly: "Proceed with your account."

"When I was brought up from the dungeon one night," continued Abram, "I was very curious to see the world and the great light of which I had heard. The house looked much the same as the cellar only neater and with better furniture; but outside — I saw the measureless space and the sky, dark but much lighter than the cellar was when the lamp was out. And so vast! I was afraid; who knew what dangers there might be lurking in the great outside.

"Then a grey light appeared from one side of the sky; soon it turned red, many shades of red, changing all the time. Then a great white light brighter than anything I had seen before. I stood and looked, I could not take my eyes away from the brightness.

"Then the sun himself rose, slowly, majestically. Fear gripped me, but trembling I was still forced to gaze at the great light, until the sun had quite risen, and I could see nothing at all anymore, so great was the light. And I threw myself upon my face and covered my eyes . . ."

There was silence in the great hall.

"You saw Shamash in his glory," said the king at last. "I begin to see why the gods wanted you to grow up in darkness. Coming out of it you saw what few men ever see, just because they have always known the light. And what happened then?"

"All that day," continued Abram, "I sat in the darkest corner I could find in the house — for the light still hurt me — and thought of what I had seen. Surely this must be the supreme god whom I had sought for so long. And yet he was different from what I had imagined. I had seen power, unimaginably great power, and even where I was sitting I could see the light and feel the great heat — but I had not seen mercy. I spoke to no one about it, fearing that they would not understand me, as they had never understood what I said of the gods, that they would get angry and call me wicked or stupid. But I kept thinking: was I wrong all that time, was the god really different from all I had felt about him? But if so, who was it that had given me life, gave me food and drink, had refreshed and healed me when I had the fever? Who was it that gave me courage and hope when I was frightened and lonely, who made me be good again when I had been angry and disobedient, who was telling me all the time, without words, that He was good and loving and that we must be good and loving like Him? This new one who possessed the great light was powerful and terrible, but he showed no mercy . . ."

"Yes," commented the king. "Shamash is mighty and terrible. I have seen, out in the desert, the bleached bones of men and beasts he had struck down in his anger. I have seen the parched lands when he was victorious over the rain god and made thousands die of famine. It is true that he is merciless in his wrath. That is why the world could not exist if other gods did not restrain him. But tell me what you decided on that day."

The hall was hushed. Priests, courtiers and soldiers were fascinated by the boy's tale, this boy who dared to have his own opinion about gods, who might be a demi-god himself — for had he not charmed Nimrod the Terrible to take his unheard-of ideas seriously?

The boy continued: "I did not find the answer that day. I sat alone and would not answer when spoken to, nor touch any food. Only when the light ceased and lamps were lit did I stop feeling afraid. In the softer light I felt more safe and peaceful, but I was exhausted. My mother gave me a cup of milk and put me to bed.

"I slept I do not know how long. When I awoke I felt cold and lonely. All was still in the house, but from afar there came from time to time strange howls and snarls, and shrieks like an evil laughter. I was so frightened that I did not dare to move or call.

"Then I noticed upon the floor near my bed a soft light; and the patch of light moved slowly until it reached me. Then I saw through the window something like a face in the sky, so soft and peaceful . . . It looked at me and seemed to say: 'Do not fear; even in the dark I am watching.'

"And I thought: this is he whom I have known in my heart, now he has come to give peace . . ."

"Nannar," said the king softly. "Nannar, the peaceful one, the merciful bringer of light in the darkness."

"But it was still cold," continued the boy. "There was still the howling and growling; and then, far worse, human cries, calling out for help, then cries of pain — and then only moaning and weeping. I said to myself: 'He is beautiful and soft, but he is weak, he does not help.' He moved away from my window and I got up and looked out after him. He was still smiling, but he did not help. And then he went lower and lower in the sky and on the other side came up the same grey light as the day before, and then the red . . . and suddenly I knew."

"What did you know?" asked Nimrod, puzzled.

"I knew that neither of them was the God I was waiting for, that both were only His servants, who must do forever the things they were given to do. They cannot help being cruel or standing by and watching cruelty. But we men — in us is the spirit of the living God, bidding us to help those in suffering and want, to defend the helpless against evil men and beasts. He who tells us this is the true God. He who made such mighty servants is mighty enough also to help us do His work. Since then I have never been afraid, but have worked and spoken for God."

The boy had finished. No one spoke. All now looked at the king; but the king had nothing to say. He beckoned to the eldest of the priests.

"Have you ever heard anything like this?" he asked him.

"Your Majesty," said the white-bearded elder. "Those men who were old when I was young used to tell that the demigods who lived long ago, before the great flood, and Utanapishtim himself who was saved from the flood and became the father of this race of men — they knew such a God of gods. But, they told us, only demi-gods can know Him, not mere men. We cannot worship One we cannot see, imagine, or understand. The gods are indeed His servants, but as the peasant must honour and obey the king's servants, and cannot hope to see the king himself, so must we mortals honour the immortals and must not try to pierce the mysteries that are not for us, lest we die. Does not a man who looks upon Shamash in his glory go blind? Is not he who defies the storm god struck down by his fierce arrow? You can see where this miserable child has been led by his overbold questing: He hankers after a God he can never know — and defies the gods he should have! Without humility, he becomes the enemy of all that is holy. He even thinks himself greater than the gods! He must repent — or he and we all will surely suffer the anger of the gods!"

Everyone breathed more easily. Here was wisdom, here was the mystery made plain!

The king himself was royal once more. "You have heard the words of the wisest of the priests," he said. "I, Nimrod, master of all men, command you to desist from these thoughts which can only bring untold harm and woe to you and anyone who might listen to you. You must never speak of these things again or you shall die. And you must, here and now, end your doubting and choose a god whom you will worship faithfully. A real god, and one visible on earth."

It was the boy's turn to look worried and perplexed. "But, your Majesty," he brought out at last, "whom can I choose? It must be someone so great that no one is greater than him, and I know nothing visible that is not subject to something greater."

"Then," claimed the king, "I will help you to choose your god. Nothing is mightier on earth than fire. Fire consumes things and men, is powerful on earth like Shamash himself on high. Serve fire!"

"But," said Abram, "fire is put out by water, so it is not supreme!"

"Well then," replied Nimrod at once, "choose water!"

"But water," continued Abram, "is sucked up by the air and carried by the wind."

"Choose the wind then," said Nimrod, "the mighty god of the storms!"

"But the wind is not supreme," argued the boy. "Men can resist the wind, and they carry the air in their lungs."

Anger had at last come to Nimrod. He stood up and shouted: "So you say that man is mightier than all? Well, worship man, worship me, the mightiest of men!"

The boy was shivering with fright, but he swallowed his tears and stammered: "But, Your Majesty, how can man be supreme? He does not live for ever!"

The king was trembling with rage, and the red vein that friend and foe had learned to fear stood out on his forehead. "Enough!" he thundered. "This evil spirit has plagued us long enough! You will not worship the gods? Then die in their honour! You refused fire, let fire be your punishment!"

He motioned the guards: "Take him to the great kiln where the bricks are made for the new chapel. Throw him into the fire!"

The guards approached the prisoner warily, for he stood fearless and erect, his eyes flashing fire. But the boy said: "Come, do your duty! Long have I worried what I could give to God who gave me everything. Now He wishes that I give my life for His glory, and I give it gladly!" Smiling he went out of the hall, surrounded by the soldiers.

Nimrod mopped his brow and the fan bearers waved their fans. "He is mad," said the king. "Possessed by an evil spirit. That is why he was able to bewitch us all at the start. But, glory be to the gods, I have broken his spell, for truth must triumph in the end."

"What do you think of my judgment?" he asked the old priest.

"Your Majesty's justice is clear as Nannar and powerful as Shamash" said the old man. "You have shown yourself truly the gods' governor on earth, valiant defender of the faith against evil men and spirits alike!"

Just then there was a commotion in the hall. The Captain of the Guards came up to the throne, running without dignity, pale as death, his eyes bulging.

"Your Majesty..." he faltered, and would have fallen if two men had not sprung to his aid.

"Your Majesty... the prisoner..."

"What, man?" asked Nimrod, staring at the soldier, "What about the prisoner?"

"Your Majesty... he walks... walks about in the kiln! The fire has not touched him! He walks, like a man walking in a garden, amongst the flames!"

"Impossible!" cried Nimrod, but he trembled. Then he rushed out of the hall. The Court streamed after him, all dignity forgotten.

There in the open kiln was the prisoner, Abram, walking happily through the fire.

Nimrod stood shaking in every limb, fighting for breath. "Come here, Abram!" he called at last.

The boy came out of the kiln and saluted the king, who shrank back from him in terror.

But the boy looked as if he hardly noticed the king. His eyes were far away. Happiness and resolution shone from his face.

"Abram," said the king, "do you hear me? Your God

exists, He has saved you. Pray Him to forgive me. You are free. Go, you and your father and all your family, but go far from here. No one shall harm you; but do not preach to us, for you are not like ordinary men!"

And they went out from Ur of the Chaldees to go to the land of Canaan; they came to Haran and stayed there.

It was there that Abram began to gather souls.

WE ATTACK AT MIDNIGHT

FROM HIS HIDING-PLACE amongst the rocks, Paltiel peered up to the sky. He knew the stars well — the old shepherd with whom he used to keep nightwatches had made him repeat their names over and over again. And the stars were the same as at Hebron — even here in the foothills of the Lebanon.

Yes, calculated the boy, in one hour it would be midnight; a fire arrow shot from the opposite hill would be the signal. And then they would charge the enemy.

The enemy! Thousands upon thousands of trained soldiers! The four combined armies of Mesopotamia! Paltiel shuddered. He was only sixteen. He had never fought men before — though he had fought jackals, and once had helped to chase a bear. But men, soldiers! His heart felt like a lump of ice.

What was it the master had said? "Anyone who is afraid can stay behind, and if we should not return he shall be free of his bond." Should he turn back? There was still time. But was he really a coward? Perhaps all the men of the tribe. now waiting in their hiding places on the hillside all round the enemy camp, had the same feeling.

Had they not all been afraid on the day of the assembly? Paltiel remembered how pale they had looked when they rose, one after another, and spoke against the plan. All the older men, bondsmen or free, the leader had asked them all. And each had said the same: "How can a small tribe of shepherds hope to win against four mighty armies."

And then Abram, their master, had spoken. "It is very hard for me," he had begun, "to order you to go to war. For years I have taught you peace and kindness to all men, friend or stranger. How can I order you now to go and kill or be killed?

"We are a small band, not even kin to each other — though the common aim unites us more strongly than ties of blood. If we should fall, there will be no one left to carry the message of God.

"And yet, because we are men of peace, because the tyrant has not attacked us ourselves, just because of that, this is our fight.

"We stand for Peace, for Justice, for Kindness. That is the way we serve the Lord of Heaven and Earth. Now this tyrant with his allies has attacked and vanquished not only his former vassals but many tribes who had done him no harm — and he has taken captive my kinsman, who is still one of us, still trying to carry on the way of God, even if he has parted company with us. He was not a citizen of the Confederation of the Five Cities but a stranger, peacefully pasturing his sheep in the open plains — and he is being taken into slavery now; and you know how they treat slaves in the two-river land.

"If we stand by and do nothing, then we shall have betrayed our duty — we shall have nothing left to live for. But if we go out and fight, not for ourselves but for Justice, then whether we live or die, we shall have done the greatest thing a man can do — we shall have offered our lives for God. Whether we live or die, humanity will be better because men have fought for Justice and not for themselves.

"Therefore, whether you obey me or not, I will go, alone if need be, and sanctify the name of God in the world with my life."

For a moment no one had moved. Then Eliezer of Damascus, the oldest and most trusted of the Master's pupils, had stood up and said: "You will not be alone, my Master, I too shall go." And then more men had called out: "And I!" "And I!" In the end everyone who was able in body had joined, three hundred and eighteen men; and the Canaanite neighbours had honoured their alliance and called out their men.

And they were still three hundred and eighteen after their long march. Not one had taken advantage of the leader's call for those overcome by fear to go home.

And should he, Paltiel, be the only one? No! He could not hope to survive the battle — but he could not desert the holy cause.

There and then he prayed to God, the Lord of Heaven and Earth, for strength and courage, and for willingness and loyalty to the end.

When the signal came he went forward joyfully and without fear, shouting "For God and Justice." The cry was taken up all around, and they charged down on the enemy. The enemy's guards made a stand whilst trumpets were blown and torches lit all over the camp. But Abram's men fought like lions. Paltiel himself struck down two of the guards, and after that he lost count. He was in the midst of the enemy, striking out right and left. He knew now that God was fighting on their side, for it had become a night of miracles. Arrows and spears hailed upon them but they were not hurt — the enemy's weapons were as harmless as straw or dust. Thousands of the enemy were slain but not one of the attackers was killed. At last the enemy fled, pursued by Abram and his men.

Paltiel stayed behind. He and the rest of the boys and old men had been told to take care of the rescued prisoners. These people were in a sorry state. They had been beaten and starved, and made to carry their own belongings for their captors. Even now they could not believe that they had been freed but thought they had merely changed masters.

The only one of them who understood what had happened was Abram's nephew, Lot, and he and his family helped them to feed and comfort the others.

Next evening the main party returned. They had pursued the enemy to near Damascus and completely scattered them. They rested the next night. Then they started on their long way back.

Their progress was slow. The freed captives, mostly women and children, were unable to march quickly. Behind them came a long train of donkeys and camels laden with the recovered loot, or carrying those who were too weak to walk. At the head of the caravan rode Abram with his rescued nephew.

Paltiel soon left them behind. He had been ordered to ride ahead and bring the news to the survivors of the Confederacy. Their kings had returned and gathered the remnants of their men. When they heard the news, there was great rejoicing. "How humble they have become," thought Paltiel, "these rich townsmen, who could only think of themselves and their money."

The news spread to all the tribes of Canaan, and delegations arrived from them all. Together they marched to meet Abram and his army. They gave him a triumphal reception and showered honours upon him. The priest-king of Salem, where the worship of the true God had survived from the days of Noah, came to greet and praise Abram.

The King of Sodom asked Abram to return to him only his people but keep the recaptured property. But Abram swore a solemn oath that he would take nothing for himself — "lest you say: I have made Abram rich."

Paltiel wondered whether the Sodomites understood what his master meant. But he, a pupil, knew exactly what made his master refuse the riches. This deed had been done for God and for Justice. It would be spoilt if they accepted a reward. Now, perhaps the Sodomites would learn that there was such a thing as kindness; perhaps they would learn to feel true gratitude.

However, when they were marching home Paltiel noticed that they had received something after all: many children from strange tribes were coming with them, to learn the way of God in the House of Abram.

THE BOY IN THE BASKET

IT WAS only mid-morning, and the day was the sixth of the third month, yet it was hotter than on a midsummer noon, and most of the children in the village had gone down to the river. But Miryam had stayed behind; sitting in the shade of the whitewashed hut, her eyes fixed on the distant hills, she was thinking . . .

She had much to think about. In her seven years — though people always said she looked and spoke like one much older — she had seen much sadness, and was trying to find out what it all meant, and how it might end.

Her father had told her the main things, of course: that God had a plan in everything, though men could not understand it until it was ripe, and even now He might be shaping things for the day when He would fulfill His ancient promise. Had He not done wonderful things to make Joseph free and mighty, even whilst his father was mourning him for dead?

A great teacher was Miryam's father. Indeed, he had come to this part of the Nile valley only to teach his poor brothers, whom Pharaoh had moved here. He himself could have stayed in Goshen, for he was of the tribe of Levi, a free man.

That was before Miryam was born. In the year she was born, Pharaoh had started to make the work so terribly hard for the Hebrews, and stopped paying them for it. That was why she had been called Miryam, her mother had told her, for Miryam meant bitterness. But she did not feel bitter. Whenever she saw some new cruelty, she would think of the glorious day when God would make them free and give them the wonderful land to live in.

Meanwhile, of course, it was hard. She often went with her mother to help people who had become ill from hard work and cruel punishments; and although she felt like crying herself, she always tried to cheer them up. "Don't despair," she might say. "Do not think of yourselves as slaves! One day we shall all be free and happy again, and then we shall know why God had to send us all this. Won't it be lovely when we'll all have our own fields and trees and houses?"

And the beaten men would smile and say: "Look at her, listen to her! Doesn't she sound like a little prophetess? Pray God that her words come true. But soon, O God, soon . . ."

And one day her father himself had called her a prophetess, in real earnest. And this was how it happened:

Three years before, just about the time her little brother Aharon was born, Pharaoh had started a most wicked and terrible thing: he ordered that all baby boys of the Hebrews were to be killed. At first he tried, secretly, to make the midwives strangle them as soon as they were born, and pretend that they had been born dead. But he soon found out that the midwives were not obeying him, so he sent his soldiers to look for new-born babies and throw them into the Nile. Anyone who tried to resist them was tortured to death.

When that happened, her father was sad and serious for many days; then he said to her mother: "I have thought long about what I have to do, and it looks to me that since I can do nothing to save the babies, I must at least see that no more are born to be killed." He had taken her mother's hands in his, and continued: "I love you dearly, Yocheved; but I must divorce you, until God shows His Mercy, and stops this bitter infliction!" And they both wept. Miryam wept too, though she hadn't quite understood what it meant. Later when he had packed his things and was going away, she ran after him and cried: "Where are you going, Daddy? Why are you going away from us?" He had picked her up and kissed her: "Don't cry, darling. I'm only going to live in the next village for a time; I have to; and you can come over every day and tell me how Mummy and baby are doing."

Yocheved had taken it quietly. "Your father," she told Miryam, "is a great and wise man. If he says it is the right thing, you can be sure that God wants it so."

But as time went on, Miryam felt more and more sure that something was wrong. She often wanted to say so to her father, but how could one tell one's father a thing like that — especially such a wise and good man as Amram?

But one day she had seen her mother handling the baby clothes that Aharon had long outgrown, and crying quietly . . . And she had understood that Yocheved was longing for another baby.

Then Miryam had become terribly excited, and run all the way to her father. Panting and flushed, she had fairly shouted at him: "You are even worse than Pharaoh! He kills the boys, but you are destroying the whole people; do you know that there is not one baby in the whole village this year. It must be because of what you have done, for people have followed your example."

She had said more then, but she hadn't known what it was, until her father had told her later. She had said: "Hear this, Amram ben Kehath: The baby that Yocheved is praying for is going to be the man who will free the Children of Israel from this place!"

But all that Miryam herself remembered was her father rocking her in his arms; when she opened her eyes, he said, ever so tenderly: "Hush, my child, calm yourself. You are right, and I was wrong. I should have trusted in God, and left it all to Him. Let His will be done."

Soon the wedding was celebrated — and a strange wedding it was, with Miryam dancing before the bride and groom, and cuddly little Aharon too with his funny steps. But soon there were many such weddings.

And three months ago the baby was born. And the moment he was born, a great light shone in the house, brighter than a summer day. Their friends saw it too, and came rushing to the cottage. They looked at the baby and said: "How good he is, anyone can see that he is good. May he bring goodness and light into this dark, evil time!"

So he was called Toviah, which meant "God is good." And Amram patted Miryam and said: "I believe that what you said about this baby will come true. It was God who spoke through you; my little daughter is a prophetess!"

She loved the baby. He was so good and so clever. They had to hide him, of course, for the Egyptians often came to see if any babies had been born. They had hollowed a niche in the wall, behind the bed-curtains, and there baby Toviah slept. He never cried, as if he understood how dangerous it was; of course he had no need to cry, for Miryam was always looking in to see if he was awake, and if she saw by the way he moved his lips that he was hungry, she took him straight to her mother.

So far all was well, thought Miryam. If only the Egyptians did not make a real search . . .

* *
*

Suddenly, Miryam became aware of running feet. A minute later, an elderly woman from the next village, a friend of Yocheved, arrived, gasping for breath. Miryam took her inside, and she told them her terrible news:

"The soldiers are in our village! Searching every house... under the beds... tapping the walls... they carry babies with them and make them cry, so that our hidden babies cry too! They say they must find every baby now, on their own lives, for this is the last search. Pharaoh's soothsayers have told him that the Hebrew leader has been born already, and they must find him. After this, they say, they will leave the babies alone.

"I don't know what you can do, but I had to tell you, and you must carry the news to your neighbours, and to the other villages. I must hurry back, and pretend I have been working in the fields, or they will torture me for telling you."

Yocheved went at once to tell the neighbours. Amram told Miryam: "This is terrible news, but do not despair. God can always help. I pray that He will grant us a plan of wisdom now. Stay with the babies until your mother comes. I shall be back soon." And he went outside, as he often did when he had to be alone with his thoughts.

Miryam was left with little Aharon, who went on playing happily with his toys, and the baby. She took him out of his hidingplace, and kissed him. She was weeping, but he smiled at her, and soon she was smiling too, and playing with him. Surely God would not forsake such a lovely, good baby!

Yocheved came back; she was frightened and weeping, but when she saw the children playing so happily, she grew calmer. "Give him to me;" she said, "let me feed him once more..." Miryam watched her feeding him, and saw her becoming restful and at peace. Indeed, she thought, in the midst of danger God sends us His peace...

Then Amram returned. There was on him a grave calm, and his eyes shone. He remained standing, and spoke slowly, quietly:

"God has answered my prayer. He has sent me good

counsel, in a strange way . . . I found myself thinking of one thing only at first, which seemed to have nothing to do with our problem: not once did the Egyptians mention drowning the children; they always say: 'put them in the river'; not: 'drown them', but: 'put them in the river' . . . Then suddenly, I knew what we must do. The safest place for our baby is — in the river . . ."

"In the river" cried Yocheved. But immediately she understood. "Oh yes! No one would look for a baby in the river. If he is hidden there, in a tiny boat, he might be safe until the search has passed . . . And this is the last search, they said . . . We might be able to pretend that he was born afterwards . . . But, oh, it is dangerous: suppose the boat overturns, and no one with him; suppose the soldiers stay a long time — he might starve. Suppose someone hears him cry . . ." And she started crying again.

Amram answered her in a soft voice: "Of course it is dangerous, my dear; but thousands are in the same danger. At a time like this we must be strong. God expects us to do the best we can think of and then to rely on Him. Let us think of how we are to do it, for there is not a minute to lose."

Yocheved pulled herself together. She brought out a basket woven of dried rushes, and made it water-proof with pitch and clay. Into it she put the baby; on top she put the lid, also of basket work, which she had not tarred, so that air could come in.

Miryam went out half-way to a quiet part of the river, and when she had signalled that no one was in sight. Yocheved hurried after her and hid the basket amongst the bulrushes, a few steps from the bank. With an effort she tore herself away, and hurried home.

But Miryam would not go away. She found a spot a little further along the river from where she could watch the boats on the river. The sun burnt down mercilessly, but she was determined to stay there until she would know what happened.

Time passed. She saw the soldiers go into the village. She prayed . . .

Suddenly, she heard the noise of many riders on the highway along the river. Soon she could make out horse-soldiers and chariots. They might be another detachment of searchers. She stepped into the water and stood between the rushes hoping she would not be noticed.

They stopped — not far from where the baby was hidden. When she looked round she saw that the soldiers had dismounted, and were forming a cordon round the area. What could this mean? Surely it was impossible that someone had betrayed them?

Then she saw a great lady stepping from a chariot. Many attendants and servant-maids crowded round her with large fans and sun shades. With them the lady walked down to the river bank. There she threw off her mantle and, clad only in light linen garments, went into the river.

"What does this mean?" thought Miryam. "A royal lady wishes to go bathing, and of all the miles and miles of river she has to choose this spot! If she comes any nearer, she will see the basket. Oh God, please, please, keep the baby safe!"

But the lady was swimming nearer; her maids walked alongside her on the bank. Now — Miryam shuddered — she had called out to them.

One after the other, several maids tried to reach the basket, but although it was quite easy to wade out to it, they all slipped and fell into the water. They could not get up, and others came to help them.

Miryam crept closer. The soldiers had not noticed her, and were now facing the outside of their square; the servants were far too busy to notice the little girl.

Now she could see the lady in the water. She was Princess Bityah, Pharaoh's daughter! Miryam had seen her in Processions.

The Princess herself had reached for the basket and opened it. Tensely, Miryam watched her. "God! " she prayed, "Even now You can help."

The baby started to cry. The Princess bent down and picked him up, and he stopped crying and smiled at her. For a while she stood with the baby in her arms, then she waded ashore. Her face had a soft and tender expression, like that of a mother holding her own baby.

When she was on the bank she turned to one of her ladies-in-waiting: "This must be one of the Hebrew babies." And she stood there playing with him.

"We must report this, your Royal Highness," said her companion. The Princess straightened up, holding the baby more firmly. "Are you giving me orders?" she asked sternly.

"Your Royal Highness will forgive her servant," replied the lady-companion, "but His Majesty has issued an order; surely those of his own house must obey him, even more than anyone else?"

No one else dared to speak, and for a moment the Princess stood still, tears in her eyes. Then she hung her head, and stumbled back into the river.

She put the baby back in his basket, and covered him. She turned to go back, but she did not go. She stayed rooted to the spot, her hand on her breast, her eyes closed. "Is she ill?" thought Miryam. What would happen now? She did not know what to pray for. Only God knew what was best now.

The Princess moved again. She took the baby back, and came to the bank. Her expression was transformed. She looked . . . thought Miryam, she looked like one who has just prayed deeply and earnestly.

Firmly she spoke to her ladies: "From to-day this child is my son. I, Bityah, so desire it!"

"Your Highness . . ." faltered the companion imploringly, kneeling to her.

The Princess spoke to her softly now: "You love me, do you not? I tell you, my life is bound up with that of this child. Something tells me that he belongs to me and I to him. It is a divine command, and whatever happens, I must obey. Come nearer and look! See what has happened to my rash!" She bared her shoulder. "You remember how bad it was this morning. How does it look now?"

The companion looked at her shoulder: "Your Highness is cured!" she said, astonished. "Healed," said the Princess, "Healed this moment by the God who watches over this child! Can I disobey Him?"

Her companion bowed deeply: "My life is yours; do what you will."

The baby began to cry. "He must be hungry," said the Princess. "Bring me my cloak!" she ordered, "And call the Captain!"

The Captain of the Guards came running up; he saluted the Princess. "You and your men," she addressed him, "have sworn me loyalty. I command you all that nothing you see here to-day shall pass your lips. Now take a chariot and fetch me a wet-nurse. — No, stay; fetch as many as you can find in the Palace. I want to choose the best." And she rocked the baby and spoke soft words to him.

Miryam was standing among the ladies now. No one took any notice of her. They were all standing round the Princess, admiring the baby.

After half an hour, the Captain returned with three nurses.

The Princess selected one, and gave her the baby; but the baby would not drink, and turned his head away. "I can't understand this," said the woman, "he is hungry, but he will not drink. Perhaps there is something about me that he does not like." But the same thing happened with the other two.

Miryam felt that she must speak now. With all the courage she could muster, she stepped forward, and knelt before the Princess. "Shall I go, Your Highness," she asked, "and call you a nursing mother of the Hebrews to suckle the baby for you?"

The Princess showed no surprise. "Yes, go!" she answered, and went on rocking the baby.

As fast as she could Miryam ran to the village and called her mother; on the way she told her what had happened. All Yocheved could say was: "Wondrous are the ways of God!"

Hiding their feelings, they came to the Princess.

"Take this baby," said Bityah, "and suckle him." He drank at once. The Princess watched tenderly. When she finished, the Princess said: "Keep him for me and nurse him, and I shall pay you well; but if you let anything happen to him, you will answer with your life."

So they took him home. Often the Princess would send for him and she loved him more and more.

Yocheved's heart was heavy when finally the baby was weaned and she had to return him to the Princess. But Miryam said: "Mother, once before I have spoken about him, and father said it was the truth. I tell you now that we are not losing him. He will remain a Hebrew and a servant of God, even in Pharaoh's Palace. Perhaps you will see a sign for it to-day."

And the last thing the Princess had to ask was: "What word do you use in Hebrew for pulling something out of the water?"

"Moshe, Your Royal Highness," answered Yocheved.

"Mo-se?" repeated the Princess. "That is a good name

in our language too. So let it be: Mo-se, for I drew him out of the water; but it was your God who told me to do it, and he belongs to Him as much as he does to me.

"I am sure he will be a good and great man one day."

HE WENT HOME

THE SUN was high over Thebes. A young man of eighteen was walking in the shade of the sycamores in the Pharaoh's Park. The ornaments in his hair and on his garment of fine byssus marked him as a Royal Prince, but he was lighter of skin and taller than Egyptians of his age, and his handsome features had a semitic shape. Birds were twittering in the trees, and from the distance came the rhythmic shouts of oarsmen on the river and the cries of children at their play, but Mose's mind was not at ease.

"Why is it," he thought, "that I am not happy? I am surrounded by luxuries, and there is no pleasure I cannot have for the asking. My Royal mother loves me as much as any real mother could, and I am a favourite of Pharaoh himself. Did he not, on my petition, grant his Hebrew slaves a weekly day of rest? Did he not banish the Midianite magician, because he was plotting against me?

"Yet I am lonely, like a man in a strange land. Yes, these people who brought me up, to whom I owe everything, even my life — in my heart they are strangers to me. Their pleasures seem childish to me — and I shudder at their cruelty. The scribes read to them about wisdom and justice — and at the same time they work the slaves to death to build them ever more marvellous monuments.

"They are so clever, so refined — but they worship their gods by behaving like savages.

"Indeed, my body-servant is happier than I, for he at least has no part in all this. He knows that he is enslaved, and can pray to the God of his fathers to redeem him."

Suddenly he stood still.

"The God of his fathers? He is the God of *my* fathers too, and I, too, though I live in a Palace, am enslaved in their evil life!"

After a moment he turned and called: "Come here, Uri!" The boy, who had been following his master at a distance, came running.

"Run to the stables," commanded Mose, "and get my Chariot. When I am gone, give my respects to my mother, and tell her I have gone for a drive in the country."

The boy bowed, and turned to carry out the order, but Mose recalled him. "One more thing, Uri. Do you love me?"

"My master," stammered the boy, tears coming into his eyes. "You have taken me from the clay pits . . . you treat me like a brother . . . there is nothing I would not do for you!"

"Would you give your life rather than betray me?" asked Mose.

"I would not betray you, my master," said Uri solemnly, "even under torture. I swear it by the God of my fathers!"

"Then," said Mose, "I am going to tell you where I am going, but don't tell any living person: I am going to visit *our* brothers and see their work."

When Uri had grasped his meaning, he almost broke down with happiness and excitement.

The Prince had called the Hebrews his brothers!

"Wait!" said Mose, "you must not go about with shining eyes. If they get suspicious they might kill us. Think of that and control yourself. Nothing has happened, and I am going for a joy ride. Have you understood? Now run!"

Soon the chariot arrived and he passed through the gate

to the salutes of the guards. He took the road to the nearest building sites.

The gilt chariot with its well greased, leather-tyred wheels, ran smoothly on the paved road. He let the thoroughbreds run as fast as they pleased. The air rushed past him, and he felt the exhilaration of speed, but it could not make him forget the seriousness of his quest.

He had visited the working-sites before, in Pharaoh's entourage, but at those times they had come to inspect the progress, or to see some newly-finished sculptures, and care had been taken that nothing should be seen that might distress some Royal Lady. The actual treatment of the slaves one could only imagine; now he wanted to see it and let himself feel — the words still sounded strange to him but he repeated them aloud — *for his brothers*.

After a time he met a column of slaves: A hundred men in single file, each carrying two hods of bricks slung from a pole, the sweat streaming down their sides. Each gang of ten had a Hebrew foreman running from man to man and exhorting them to keep up the pace. One gang broke its order, and it was the foreman who tasted the whip of the Egyptian overseer.

When Mose reached them he stopped, and at an order from the Egyptian, the column stopped too. Mose ordered the overseer to give them a pause for rest, whilst he would inspect them, and they put down their loads and sat by the roadside.

Mose questioned the overseer about such things as the places between which they transported the bricks, and how many journeys they made in a day. Then he told him he wished to inspect the men alone.

He walked along the line. The men were slumped on the ground, silent and listless. So this was what slavery had made of people who could have been as lively and quick-witted as Uri or himself!

He stopped in front of a young man who seemed more alert than the rest. The man stood up and bowed.

"What treatment do you receive?" Mose asked him.

The man averted his eyes as he answered: "The will of Pharaoh is carried out correctly, as my lord can see."

Mose made another attempt: "Have your people always been slaves?"

At this the man straightened himself, and clenched his fists: "Our fathers were free men, and one day we shall be free again, in a land of our own!"

Then he realised that he was speaking to an Egyptian and a noble, and he added: "Forgive me, my lord, I forgot myself. I am in your hands." And he threw himself on his face.

Mose found it hard to contain his pity. A people once free and proud, and now brought so low. *A* people? *His* own people!

"Stand up," commanded Mose. "I will not punish you, or tell anybody; but only if you tell me all you know. How did your servitude begin, and when?"

The man looked up at him in surprise. Then he stood up, and began, hesitating at first, then forcefully.

"May God remember you this mercy, my lord. Pharaoh declared us slaves before I was born, but my father was a grown man. We kept our sheep in the land of Goshen, which a Pharaoh had given us for great services. Then there was an invasion and our men fought bravely for Pharaoh. When we had driven out the enemies. Pharaoh called all his peoples to build fortresses against the enemy's return. Our people went, all but the tribe of Levi, and worked together with the Egyptians, as free labourers for good pay. The Egyptians gradually went home, but the soldiers did not let us go, and then they stopped paying us. Pharaoh had proclaimed us slaves!"

So that was how it had come about, thought Mose. Not a slave people were his fathers, but free men made prisoners by a trick! But he went on:

"Why do you go on worshipping a God who does not help you?"

"Our God," answered the man with dignity, "is mighty. He did great wonders for our forefathers, and He promised them the land of Canaan for their descendants. But first, said God, we must be strangers and slaves for many years. And so it came to pass; but we trust in God that as this came true so will the rest."

Mose became aware of the overseer hovering uneasily at a distance. He understood the man's fears, and stepped back, signalling him to proceed. At a shout of command the slaves resumed their order and shouldered their loads.

The overseer helped Mose into the chariot and saluted him. The slave who had been holding the horses stood back and Mose drove off — to the brick works of which the overseer had told him.

He thought over what he had seen. The dumb resignation of the slaves had affected him more deeply even than the sufferings he had imagined; but the spirit of the man, once it had been awakened, had both increased his pain and given him comfort. If they were all like that man, remembering what freedom meant, then there was still hope.

He found himself calculating the chances of a succesful revolt, if they could find a leader — and realised with a shock that he was already a traitor — no, not a traitor, but an enemy of Pharaoh.

The brickworks were now in sight. He could see the stacks of finished bricks, the slaves bringing up the clay, kneading it, moulding the bricks. But there was one thing that held his eye, and that made him whip the horses to their utmost speed.

An overseer was furiously hitting a man, who was down already, hitting him again and again with all his might.

Mose brought the chariot to a skidding stop, making the horses rear up. "Stop this!" he shouted at the surprised Egyptian, before even dismounting. "Why are you beating this man so hard?" he demanded sharply.

The overseer, still panting from his exertions, took time to answer. Then he said, pompously: "My lord, this slave is rebellious, and refuses to obey orders. He were better dead and an example to the rest."

"And what do *you* say?" Mose asked the Hebrew, who was painfully picking himself up. The man's body was covered with weals, and there was blood on his face.

"My lord," he brought out slowly, "I have done no wrong. But I am the only witness of a terrible crime this overseer committed this morning, and he wants to kill me to cover it up." And he told him what he had seen.

"The slave is lying...!" began the Egyptian; but when he saw Mose, he stopped and shrank back. For a holy fire was burning in the young man's eyes.

"I can see who is lying!" he said. "For what you have done you doubly deserve death. May the God of the Hebrews punish you!" And he raised his fist and struck the man full in the face.

The Egyptian crumpled under the blow, fell and lay still, his eyes staring at the sky.

Mose turned to the trembling Hebrew. "Your God has avenged you. Have no fear; no man is here but your brothers, and they will not betray us. I shall hide the body, and if you are asked, say that he walked away and did not return. Help me put him on the chariot."

When this was done Mose drove into the nearby desert and buried the body in the sand.

He turned for home, bewildered and elated at the same time. One day had changed him from Pharaoh's favourite into a champion of the Hebrews. For from now on he was fighting for them; the decision had been sealed in blood. He felt no sin for killing the guilty man. He was sure it was the will of God.

He did his best to conceal his change of heart under the stiff, pompous pose that was fashionable. He did not tell even Uri what had happened.

Next morning he drove out again, this time to a building site. The place was full of furious activity: brick-layers and their supply gangs, sculptors pounding away at statues, long chains of slaves dragging blocks of stone on sledges, overseers, architects . . .

The official in charge was somewhat confused by having an unannounced inspection; but Mose explained that his visit was not official. He just wanted to watch the work, and he needed no guide. He managed to convince the official that he really was not wanted.

Mose strolled round the place looking for a chance to get into conversation with a Hebrew. He saw a gang sitting down to a hasty meal, and went over to them. Again he noticed that he could walk right in front of them without their taking notice. But suddenly he heard behind him angry voices. He turned and saw two Hebrew foremen involved in an argument. The Hebrew he had learned from Uri was not quite enough to follow their rapid exchanges, but it seemed to be about whose gang was more efficient.

Suddenly one of them raised his hand to strike the other. Hurrying to them Mose called out: "Stop! why should you hit your own brother?"

Both of them turned to him, and the one who had started to fight measured him with a defiant look. Then he folded his arms and said maliciously: "And who made you an official and judge over us? Perhaps you'd like to kill me, as you killed that Egyptian?"

Mose was dumbfounded. He had not expected that the Hebrews might not want his sympathy. Also he was afraid; there was an overseer sitting quite near, and he might have understood the words. He turned away, the two men's laughter ringing in his ears, and went to his chariot.

He was on his way home before the thought struck him. "So the thing is known!" he exclaimed. If it had spread to another site, many people must already know both his act and his description. And if that man dared to defy a Royal Prince, it could only mean that Pharaoh knew too, or would know very soon. If he went home, he would be going to certain death.

If he was to live to do anything for the Hebrews, he must go amongst them now, both to hide himself and to meet their Elders. Perhaps even now the time was ripe for an uprising!

It was then that his true plight struck him with its full sickening force: If there were Hebrews who could betray one who helped them, he was not safe amongst them. What was worse: as long as they were like that it was useless to fight for them: Their God would surely not save them. Yesterday he had found his people — had he lost them to-day?

He must flee. He would go into the desert, live the life of an outlaw. Perhaps later on he could lose himself in a strange country or take service in some foreign army.

He searched his memory for a place where he could hide. There were some Burial Cities of long ago, now surrounded by desert and neglected, where fugitive criminals went into hiding. Which of them was nearest?

* It was then he noticed that he had lost his bearings. Whilst he was thinking, the horses had taken him off his route . . .

* *

*

A village grew out of the horizon. In this outlying place they might not know of the search yet — if indeed it had begun. He would ask the way to Thebes, and from that find out where he was.

In the village, he came upon an elderly woman. She was a Hebrew, but from her unhurried, graceful walk he could see she was not of the slaves.

He reined in near her. Then he saw her face . . . It was a face long familiar to him, though he could not remember having met her. It was a face he had seen in dreams; it was how he imagined his mother.

He sprang from the chariot and addressed her: "Who are you, mother?"

This was the way the Hebrews addressed elder women. But she stared at him as at a ghost. With an effort she recovered herself and answered respectfully:

"My name is Yocheved, my lord, a daughter of Levi."

"Yocheved?" he knew that name! "Did you ever serve at Pharaoh's court?" No, that could not be it. "Did you once nurse a baby for Princess Bityah?"

She could not answer; she had begun to weep. But that was answer enough. He embraced her. "You are my old nurse!"

She restrained him. "My lord," she said tearfully, "when I returned you to the Princess, I had to promise never to try to see you! We must not incur the Pharaoh's anger!"

* Regarding the rest of this story, see appendix.

"Pharaoh?" asked Mose with bitterness. "I am now fleeing from Pharaoh, fleeing for my life!"

Yocheved cried out in terror. Then she put her arms round him. "What has happened, my poor son? Have I not suffered enough in giving away my child?"

Mose was stunned. "Your child? Are you my true mother? Oh, say it is true!" She could only nod and he went on: "Praise be to God who has shown me my mother before it is too late. Does my father live? Have I brothers and sisters? . . ."

Then he realised that people had begun to crowd round them.

It must not be known that he had stayed here. At least there were no Egyptians among them. He explained, in Hebrew, that they must keep his arrival a secret, or else the whole village might be punished. "Don't look at my dress!" he concluded, "I am a true son of Israel!"

"And *my* son, brothers!" added Yocheved. "Please, my brothers, give him shelter in our village."

A man came forward to take the reins, and Mose asked him to hide the chariot and tend to the horses, for he would leave again soon.

His mother took him to her cottage. He embraced his father Amram, a saintly elder, and his brother Aharon, a learned young man full of love for God and Man. Later Miryam came in, the sister who had helped to save his life.

Later, over the food, he told them of his life at Court, his experiences and his present danger. They listened, and questioned him, with love and understanding. For the first time in his life he felt at home.

"How I wish I could stay with you!" he exclaimed at last.

Yocheved swallowed her tears, and answered: "You will

always be with us, my son, for now you are suffering with us, and for us!"

His father added: "You will escape this danger, my son, for you fought for God, and He will help you. But when you are in exile, in strange countries, it will be your difficult duty not to forget your God and your people."

Then he told him of the Patriarchs, and of God's promises and commands. Finally he said: "Maybe you will be able one day to come back and help your brothers. But you have much to learn first: to seek nothing for yourself, and all for God; to strive to improve your brothers, yet to love them, with all their faults. Above all, humility and patience, for you cannot change men in one lesson, and you cannot teach them at all if you seek power or honours for yourself.

"Look out for these things, and learn them from whatever trials God will send you. When you will have learnt enough, God will show you what you have to do."

These words remained with Mose when he set out on his wanderings.

THREE HUNDRED MEN

IT WAS getting dark in the cave — that mountainside cave which had served as home for the whole town every summer for years, ever since the Midianites, the raiders from the desert, had started coming. Gideon son of Yoash was having trouble persuading Yether, his eldest boy, to go to sleep.

"I'm so hungry, Daddy!" said Yether. "And I can't eat any more of those dried dates; they make me so sick. Can't you get us some more bread?"

Gideon exchanged a look with his wife. Yes, the flour was all used up, and no grain left to make more. He hadn't been able to bring much last time.

"Go to bed now, Yether," he answered his first-born, "and to-morrow, if God wills, you shall have fresh matzoth."

He tried to persuade his servant to go with him, but the man refused to stir from the cave. Only today a troop of Midianites had passed in the valley; the last time they had been here, only a week earlier, they had caught a group of men in the fields and made them prisoners, amongst them Gideon's own brothers.

When it was fully dark, Gideon went down to the farm all alone, to get some barley for his family.

To have to go into their own fields like thieves in the night! And this was the seventh summer that Midian had come. How would it end, how long could one live like that? Each year more of them came, each year less food was left for Israel.

He reached the barley fields. They were bare! The enemy

had been here before him! All the barley gone! And the wheat was far from ripe. He would have to get some wheat just the same, and they would dry it over the fire. Some of the wheat had been cropped and trampled by the marauders' animals, but a lot was still there. He cut as much as he could before dawn, and carried it uphill to the vineyard. He hid it in the wine-press, which was in a shelter hewn in the rock. The enemy was not likely to come into the vineyard this early in the year.

When he had brought in the last load, he started threshing. It was slow and difficult work threshing fresh, unripe wheat with a flail — in peacetime he had merely to stand on the threshing-sledge and drive the ox — but hard or easy, he had to bring home some grain.

The sun had risen, when he felt that someone was watching him. He peered out — keeping in the shade of the wine-press entrance. No one to be seen. But wait — under that tree . . . A moment ago he hadn't see anything there, but now — yes, there was a man, sitting quite still, looking at him . . . Gideon felt uneasy. How had the man got there so suddenly — if he was a man and not some kind of spirit? But he felt he had to go to him. Still the man did not move; but when Gideon had come quite near him, the man lifted his hand and spoke: "God with you, mighty warrior!"

The words might have been just a greeting, but Gideon felt that this was no ordinary man, and that the words had a special meaning. His bearing and the way he spoke reminded Gideon of the prophet who had recently spoken in the village, blaming the troubles on the people's sins. But why call him, who was this moment hiding from the invaders, a mighty man? And was God with them just now?

"Please, my master," he answered," is God with us? Then why has all this come upon us? And where are all His miracles of which our fathers have told us, saying 'Indeed God has taken out of Egypt?' And now He has left us, and delivered us into the hand of Midian?"

Then a strange feeling came over Gideon: He heard the words he had just spoken echoing round him, as if all Israel were asking "Why has God forsaken us?" And he felt a deep sorrow, but no longer was he sorry for himself and his family. That was forgotten in the sorrow of Israel, and with this change came strength and courage. The words he had spoken to the prophet half in anger had become a prayer to God, a prayer that was sure to be answered.

And now came a feeling unlike anything he had ever known: a feeling of awe in a mighty presence, but without terror, a clearness as if daylight had become many times stronger and he many times more awake, yet he could no longer see the things around him.

Then came the voice: "Go, with this strength of yours, and save Israel from the hand of Midian; in truth, I have sent you!"

Then there was silence.

Gideon was trembling. He help Israel? He, who could not help himself? He, a young farmer whose voice had never yet been heard in the village council, who had never worn arms or commanded free men?

It seemed impossible, but if God would help him nothing was impossible.

"Oh, please, my God!" he cried. "With what can I help Israel? See, my 'thousand' is the poorest in Manasseh, and I myself the youngest man in my clan!"

But he felt courage flooding into him, even as the voice answered:

"Because I will be with you, you will beat Midian like one man."

But how was he to convince the people that God had indeed spoken to him? Would he himself believe it tomorrow, or would he think of it as a strange dream? He must have a visible sign, at least some action by which he could prove to himself that he was not dreaming.

The prophet was still sitting where he had first seen him. Gideon asked him to wait until he could prepare a gift. He took the grain he had threshed to the cave — he was not afraid now to be out in daylight — and in less than an hour he was back, with a basket of hot matzoth and a pot of goat-kid's meat.

The man told him to put the bread and meat on a rock, and pour the gravy over them. Then he touched them with his staff. A flame leapt out of the rock and burned up the offering! The man had disappeared.

Then Gideon knew that he had seen not a prophet, but an Angel of God, and he was afraid, for did not people say that one who had seen an Angel must die?

But he heard the voice of God: "Peace to you, do not fear. You will not die."

Gideon bowed down. Then he collected stones and built an altar on that spot, which he called "God is peace."

All day he went about deep in thought. What was his duty now, and would he really be able to do what God had commanded?

In the night the voice came again, commanding him to break up the altar of Baal, cut down the tree that was held sacred to the Asherah, and build an altar to God on top of the mountain. He was to take the bull which his father had kept through all these seven years, the bull dedicated to Baal, and sacrifice it to God, burning it on the new altar, with the wood of the tree he had cut down.

So this was to be his first task, to defy the idol-worship in which most of the people believed! He would do it too, even if they would kill him for it; but if they knew in advance they would stop him before he could do it.

He commanded ten servants to come with him, and this time he was obeyed. By morning everything had been carried out.

But hardly had he come home, when people were assembling outside, demanding his blood. Gideon's father himself, as head of the town, was called upon to pronounce his punishment. But when he had heard what Gideon had to say, he told the people: "Are you going to defend the Baal? If he is a god, let him fight for himself!"

And looking at Gideon facing them fearlessly and full of holy zeal, the people became doubtful, and accepted his father's judgment. They called Gideon "He whom Baal will fight," but as nothing happened to him, they finally went away, saying: "Maybe Baal is just a foolishness after all!"

After this, people respected Gideon and listened to his speeches, in which he told them to leave idol-worship, which had brought on them oppression, and pray to God, who alone could help them.

The enemy must have heard that there was a stirring amongst the Israelites, for they collected their forces and went down into the valley-plain of Yezreel, cutting off the northern tribes from the rest of Israel.

Gideon felt the spirit of God on him. He went up to the mountaintop and blew the war signal with the Shofar. Every able man in the clan of Avi-Ezer came to his camp. Then he sent heralds through the rest of the land of Manasse, and the people came. He sent westward into Asher, Zebulun and Naftali, and marched out to meet their contingents.

He now had a sizeable army; still, they were few indeed against those battle-trained hordes from the deserts. But Gideon told his men to rely on God's help. To show them that

God was with them he prayed for a public sign. He took a fleece of wool and left it in the open overnight. In public, he asked God that in the night dew should fall only on the wool whilst the earth around should be dry; the next night he prayed for the opposite, that the wool alone should remain dry.

Both signs arrived, and the whole army acclaimed God. Early that morning Gideon gave the command to break camp, and to move into battle position on the hill by the spring Harod, opposite the enemy.

But before he could begin the fight, God spoke to him:

"The men with you are too many that I could give Midian into your hand. Israel might boast: 'My own hand has saved me!' "

He was to address the army and command that anyone who felt afraid should go home during the night.

Gideon was troubled, but he knew that he had to obey. Next morning, 22,000 of his men had left. Only 10,000 remained, but since God wanted it, it must surely be for the better.

But again God told him he had too many men. He was to send them down to the brook to drink and to watch them. Those who knelt down to drink he should stand apart. There were only 300 who had not knelt.

Then God commanded him to send home every one except those 300. With these He would save Israel.

Gideon obeyed, but he could not understand how he was to go into battle with his small troop against the mighty army that he saw encamped below him in the valley.

Evening came, and he went to his tent with a troubled mind. But in the night God spoke to him: "Get up, and attack the camp, for I have delivered it into your hands.

"But if you are afraid to attack, go down to the camp with only your boy Poora. Hear what they are talking, and your hands will be strengthened; then you will attack."

Gideon rose, and with Poora, went cautiously down to the enemy. The camp looked even larger than from the top of the hill, the tents seemed to stretch endlessly. Halfway down, he saw the kneeling camels, hump to hump, and tried to count them. But he gave up; they seemed like the sand on the beach.

They crept up to the outposts. Hiding in the shadow of a tent, Gideon could hear two sentries talking.

One of them was telling a dream he had had before he was awakened for duty. He had seen a barley cake rolling through the camp. It reached his tent, pushed it over and turned it upside down.

After a while the other sentry answered: "That means the sword of Gideon Ben Yoash, the Israelite. God has given Midian into his hand!"

When Gideon had heard this he bowed to God. Then he went back to his camp as fast as he dared and aroused his men.

He split them into three equal groups. Each man was to carry a Shofar, and a burning torch hidden in an empty jug. He gave them their instructions.

By different routes they crept up to the enemy camp. When they were placed around it — it was just the beginning of the middle watch, and they could hear the changing of the sentries — Gideon and his detachment blew their Shofaroth and smashed the jugs; immediately the other groups did the same. Every man held up the torch in his left hand and the Shofar in the right. They shouted their battle cry "For God and Gideon!" but they did not advance.

The enemy sounded the alarm, but God had sent confusion into them. They ran about in disorder. Again the Shofaroth sounded, and the enemy thought it was nearer. Seeing their own men outlined against the blaze of torches, they took each other for enemies. They began fighting each other furiously. Finally they ran for the camels, and fled in disorder. Gideons' men had not even drawn their swords.

Quickly Gideon sent messengers into Ephraim, and their men occupied the Jordan in time to kill or capture many of the enemy, and two of their tribal chiefs. He alerted the tribes of Naftali, Asher and Manasseh and they harassed the fleeing columns.

Gideon himself pursued the main enemy group. Eventually, deep in Trans-Jordan, he caught up with them. With 15,000 men the remaining two leaders had re-formed their camp. 120,000 had fallen on the way.

In another surprise attack he dispersed the camp and captured the leaders. When it was found that they had murdered the hostages, they were executed.

Midian did not trouble Israel again, and for forty years there was peace.

But when all Israel asked Gideon to become their King, his answer was:

"I will not rule you, nor shall my son rule you. Let God be your ruler!"

THE GIRL FROM MOAB

THE SUN was going down over the hills in the west far away across the crystal mirror of the Sea of Salt. It had been a hot day for this early season, but now a cooler breeze was blowing and Ruth was glad to sit outsidc, glad to be alone. Her sister-in-law Orpah had gone to milk the goats and Ruth was pleased to be rid of her chatter, glad to be able to think.

The world was such a strange place; nothing went right for long. Or perhaps it was she who was strange — Orpah seemed to be quite happy, even now . . .

Yes, they had called her a strange one, even when she was a girl. She never went to have fun with the boys as everybody else did. Even when she had to go to the dancing on festivals she shrank from the touch of the men and had wondered how all the wild things that were done there could be called holy and pleasing to the gods.

She had only had one real friend — not counting Orpah who had only been a hanger-on to her. And that was a strange thing too, for Naarah was a slave girl, a captive whom Ruth's father had brought back from a raid into the Reuben country. Naarah was a slave and a stranger, she spoke with a funny accent and did many strange things: she would not eat meat, and one day every week she refused to work until she was beaten — yet somehow that very strangeness had attracted Ruth to her. Perhaps it was just because she too was different from everybody. But Ruth thought that somehow the poor slave girl was better and wiser than anyone else she knew. So she spent a lot of time with her and loved to hear her tell of her home and of her people — and of her God. A strange God He was too; Ruth never understood all about Him. Apparently no one could see Him, He wasn't made of stone or even of gold, in fact, you couldn't find Him anywhere — or as Naarah said so strangely, He was everywhere; and He didn't allow His people to have any other God. He punished them very much if they did wrong. All very strange and terrifying, but at least this God told the people what was right and what was wrong; not like Kemosh and the other gods who let the people do what they liked and then suddenly got angry and had to be appeased with harsh and cruel things, such as sacrificing children — and that didn't always help.

Yes, the Israelite tribes were strange people, and yet Ruth loved to hear about them, for some of the things they called wrong were those that Ruth herself hated. But in the end her father had had enough of Naarah's tricks and sold her back to her own people. For a long time Ruth had been very lonely.

* *
*

Then the people from Judah came, an elderly couple with two sons. They had been rich and honoured in their own country, anyone could see that. Everyone respected them, even Ruth's own family who were so proud of their descent from King Eglon. The strangers had brought money with them and bought land and cattle and built a house. Of course, they did not take part in the Moabite festivals, and some people disliked them for it, and said it was unlucky to have too much to do with them. But Ruth knew all about these special ideas of the Israelites and liked to visit them; Orpah, who copied Ruth although she was so different, often went too.

The old man, Elimelech, used to grumble at his sons when they spent too much time with the girls, but Naomi, the mother, liked them and taught them many things. After a time it was taken for granted that the girls could come whenever they liked. Ruth saw the strange things actually done and she liked them; in fact, she was only really happy when she was with the Judah people, and she began to wish she were one of them. And then the old man died. He left very little of the riches he had possessed — most of them had been used up.

After that the girls became even more friendly with the family. Machlon fell in love with Ruth. Naomi wept and begged him not to marry her — so very strange it seemed after being so good to her — but Machlon insisted. Kilyon took the part of his brother, and in the end they married. Later, Orpah married Kilyon.

How she had loved Machlon, and what a good husband he had been, so gentle and considerate, not like the men of Mo'ab at all. He had never once hit her, and whenever they quarrelled he was soon ready to make it up. She had thought that now at last she was one of Israel; she had looked forward to the day when she would be a mother in Israel . . .

But she never had a child. And as time went on she had sometimes watched Machlon in unguarded moments, and had seen in his face, in his eyes, that something was wrong, that there was something between them. But every time, when he had seen her sadness, he just said something to make her laugh. He never told her what was wrong; never, until the end ...

In the end, when he was ill, when he knew he was going to die of the plague that had taken Kilyon and many Moabites, he told her. She had been sitting up with him, doing what she could to ease his pain; and suddenly he said:

"Ruth, my darling, you know that I am going to die.

I have asked God to forgive my sins, but I must ask your forgiveness too. It is my fault that you are left a young widow . . ."

She had tried to comfort him but he went on:

"We should never have left the Holy Land. True, there was a famine, but we were not starving yet; we only went away to avoid sharing with the poor what we had left. God is just; we sinned. But my own sin was that I married you, for we must not marry one who is not in the covenant of God — even if she is as good as yourself."

"But why didn't you tell me! " she cried. "I would gladly have come into your covenant! "

"It would have been no good if you had done it merely in order to marry me. Perhaps now you are willing to join us in truth, but I could not know it then. Besides, you are a Moabite . . . Anyway, it is too late. May God, who sees the heart and does not punish the innocent, repay you for your suffering . . ."

And now Machlon was dead, Naomi heartbroken and sad. She insisted on calling herself Marah, the bitter one, instead of Naomi, the pleasant one, and was always weeping for her and her family's sins Most of all she wanted to go home, to die on holy soil . . .

If Naomi went Ruth would not stay. She would go with her, or if necessary, follow separately. Rather be a stranger in Israel than at home in Mo'ab . . .

But would she be admitted into Israel? What had Machlon meant when he said: "Besides you are a Moabite . . ."? Did that mean she could not go into Israel? She got up and rushed into the house. She found Naomi putting things into a basket.

"Mother dear," asked Ruth, "Is it true that Moabites can't become Israelites?"

Naomi straightened up. "Who told you that? Of course they can come into the covenant. Anybody can who is completely sincere. What Moabites can't do is to *marry* Israelites, even after they have come into our faith.

"That is why I didn't want my sons to marry here. If only they had listened to me! They would still be alive, and you and Orpah would be happy with husbands and children of your own people . . ." And she wept.

Ruth took hold of Naomi gently. "Listen to me, mother. I don't know about Orpah, but you needn't pity me. I shall never marry a Moabite. I want to stay with you, and if you go home I shall go with you, and join the faith of Israel, even if I never get married again! "

Naomi looked at her with love and pity. "My dear child, you don't know what it means. Maybe it looks good to you from here, but you have never been away from home. You don't know what it means to be a stranger, particularly for a lonely poor woman. My family will look after me, but you would have to go picking up what the harvesters had left in the fields, and in winter you might have to go begging. As for joining the faith, it is harder than you think to keep all the Commandments. If you stay as you are and keep the seven commandments given to Noah you will be better off than if you joined Israel and afterwards did not keep the Torah.

"No, Ruth, I have thought it over carefully. It will be hard for me to part from you, but it is better this way. I am packing now. Tomorrow at dawn I am leaving. I have made enquiries. God has remembered His people; there is a fine crop of barley, and the wheat is coming along well. I shall not suffer want at home. You and Orpah can keep all that is left of the property, so I hope you will manage until you get married again."

* *
*

Ruth had not given way, and Orpah too had insisted on coming along. Poor Orpah, she didn't know what was good for her. She really ought to have stayed. Had she not often told Ruth how she missed the fun and dances? This would have been her chance to go back to her old ways, but no matter what Ruth and Naomi said to her, she had to do what Ruth did.

Today was their third day on the road. Each day Naomi had urged them to turn back and they had refused. They were in Reuben country now and the road was beginning to drop into the Yarden Valley. Suddenly Naomi stopped . . .

"Please, my daughters go, return to your mothers! May God do kindness with you, as you have done with the dead and with me. May God grant that you find rest each of you in her husband's house." She kissed them and turned to go.

But the girls cried aloud and said: "We want to go back with you to your people!" Again, Naomi said: "Turn back my daughters. You ought to get married again, and if you go with me you will stay unmarried and poor. It is much worse for me than for you, for God has punished me!" They all wept together.

At last Orpah kissed Naomi and returned home. But Ruth stayed.

"Look," said Naomi, "there goes your sister-in-law; she is going back to her people — go back with her!"

But Ruth answered: "Do not urge me to leave you, to turn back from you. Where you go, I will go. Where you sleep, I will sleep. Your people are my people, your God is my God! Where you will die I will die, and there I will be buried. I swear by the God of Israel that only death shall separate me from you!"

When Naomi saw that she was determined she said no more about it. Later she told her why she had refused so long. It was usual to refuse a stranger for three days before accepting him into the covenant, to make sure he was sincere. Now that she had passed the test she could appear before the Elders as soon as they reached Beth-Lechem, to declare her faith. Then she would immerse herself in the Mikveh and afterwards she would give a sacrifice to be offered up on the Altar.

* *
*

It had been a sad homecoming. Even Naomi's own family were hardly able to recognise her, so much had she changed in the sad time she passed in Mo'ab; and all were sad to hear of Elimelech's family dying out.

But they had not suffered want. Naomi's family had given her a little cottage to live in, and Ruth had gone to the fields to pick after the harvesters.

And God had been with her, for the very first field she went to belonged to a man called Bo'az who was a cousin of Machlon, though he was much older. He had told her to come to his fields every day and to have her lunch with his servant girls. He must have told his men to drop sheaves on purpose, for she was barely able to carry home all that she found. When the barley harvest was over they had started on the wheat, and by now Ruth and Naomi had grain to last them for more than a year, and they had sold some and bought a goat and things they needed.

Now it was winnowing time, and Bo'az had invited Ruth to come to the party he would give for his workers when the work was finished and the Priest's gift had been lifted from the heap of clean grain.

But Ruth sat around at home. She did not feel like going to any parties. The kindness Bo'az had shown her had made her happy and thankful, but now that the rush of harvest was over and she had time to think, this only made her more unhappy. What good was it to be treated well, the same as any Israelite girl, when she must not marry into the tribe — marry, for instance, such a man as Bo'az himself, whom she adored and who seemed to like her too . . .

Still she could not complain. This was what she had wanted. And one could not compare it with life in Mo'ab. Suddenly Naomi came in, all flushed and excited: "Aren't you dressed yet?" she asked.

"I am not going, mother," answered Ruth, "I am not in the mood for a party."

"Hush, my daughter," replied Naomi, "you must listen to me now. I have been looking for some time to find you a home. I want you to wash and anoint yourself, and put on your Shabbath dress. Go to the threshing place for the party, but keep out of Bo'az sight until all the eating and drinking is over and they go to sleep on the straw. Then seek him out, wake him up and tell him you would like him to marry you. He will be only too happy, I am sure. I know he likes you, and he is a relation and ought to look after the family."

"But —" stammered Ruth, "didn't you tell me I could never marry an Israelite? — or was that only part of putting me off?"

"No," answered Naomi, "I really thought so then. We all did. But after we came back I heard that the prophets had been here and taught us an oral law which had been forgotten. They said they knew positively that only men of Ammon and Mo'ab are forbidden to marry Israelite women, but that a Moabite woman, like you, can marry any man of Israel. The people are not used to the idea yet, but Bo'az is a learned man. He will be only too glad to be the first to demonstrate the law, and the Elders will back him up."

"I will do all you say, mother dear!" said Ruth, and she hurried to get ready.

All went as Naomi had said. Bo'az was glad she had come to him and praised her for it. And the Elders praised him, and they blessed them, saying: "May God make this woman who is coming into your house like Rachel and Leah, who both built the house of Israel!"

So they married. The following year Ruth had a son whom she called Oved, the servant, for she wanted him to be a true servant of the God of Israel.

Naomi was so happy that she became like a young woman again; she always carried the baby around, until it became a joke in town: "Naomi has had a baby!"

That was Oved, who became the father of Yishai, whose son was David, King of Israel.

THE BEGINNING

"RABBI," SAID THE YOUNG MAN SUDDENLY, when his teacher paused in his explanations, "forgive me, but I cannot follow your lesson any more today." And he hid his face in the folds of his Tallith.

They were sitting in the garden of the Rabbi's house on the hillside. Below them lay the great city of Shushan; the Jews' market was immediately under where they sat. On the opposite hill, over terrace upon terrace clad in the fresh green of springtime, the Royal Palace stood gleaming in the light of the setting sun, and the music of the King's entertainment reached them muffled by the distance.

The King loved parties, but tonight — the grapevine had it — he was entertaining the Prime Minister after an important audience. A new law had been discussed, and there were wild speculations. Some said the recent tax cuts would be cancelled, some said they would be extended. In the market below them traders were still running to and fro. But it was not the market that worried the student.

The white-robed Rabbi, a look of compassion on the gentle face framed in a flowing white beard, spoke softly to his pupil: "I have noticed, Shaltiel, that you are not at ease. But won't you tell me what oppresses you? Perhaps I can help you — and it will ease your mind to speak of what is disturbing you."

The young man looked up. Deep sorrow lay in his delicate features. "How can I speak" he began. "The Prophet

Yecheskel has said in the name of God: 'Can my ways not be understood? Indeed it is your ways that cannot be understood.' How then can I speak? What oppresses my mind, what prevents me from giving attention to your teaching, concerns the ways of God!"

"Nevertheless," the teacher said softly, "Perhaps together we shall find some answer to your problem."

Hesitatingly the youth began: "You were speaking, my master, of the laws of the Temple. You were speaking in the present tense 'here stands the Altar, there are the stairs to the Temple' as if the Holy Temple were standing. But it has been in ruins for two generations! How can I learn about this without being oppressed by our cruel shame?"

"Explain yourself, my son," said the master. "Your pain is creditable though nevertheless it is our duty to study the laws of the Temple; not only so that we shall know them, when the time comes, as assuredly it will, to rebuild it, but also so that meanwhile our yearning for the full worship of God, and our occupation with its laws, shall fill the place of the missing service. But why call it a shame, and why cruel?"

"I did not mean to speak, my master — do you wonder that my words are not fit to be spoken? But what other words can I give it?

"Since King Yechonyah and the cream of our nation were taken to Babel, much more than the 70 years foretold have passed, but still the Temple is in ruins. It is true that Cyrus allowed the Jews to return but his permission to build the Temple was soon revoked, and to this day the offerings at Jerusalem are brought on an Altar without the Temple standing behind it. Can one then understand the ways of God?

"What is to become of us? Instead of weeping at our fate we do business and grow fat. The resettlement of Jerusalem and Yehudah, our pride and our hope, has become our shame. Noblemen marrying heathen women! The Shabbath desecrated in public! Are we to disappear amongst the nations of the Empire?

"And here in Shushan? Jews at the King's public feasts, a Jew at Court, and now — secret though it is — a Jewish Queen!

"How long can we last like this? We have atoned for the old sins, as the Prophets said, but instead of the glorious return — this!

"What else can I call it but shame, what else but cruel!

"We are drifting I know not whither. The Rabbis warned, preached — but who listened? Ever since we were granted equality with all nations, things have been getting worse and worse. We keep the laws at home, but many of us deny their spirit in public. And God watches and is silent — can His ways be understood?"

He had stood up and spoken ever more fiercely, but when he had finished he collapsed into an attitude of hopelessness. For some minutes he stared across at the Palace, as if forgetful of the presence of his teacher.

Suddenly he pulled himself together. He turned to the teacher: "Rabbi, am I out of my mind? Is it wild and witless what I spoke — what I think day and night? — What shall I do?"

"Be calm, my son," the Rabbi said in a voice full of deep compassion. "You said some words that you already regret, but a man is not judged by what he says while in pain, and your pain stems from love of God and His people...

"Sit down with me and let us search for the answer, for answer there is to every question asked by one who seeks divine truth.

"What does the Prophet mean when he says: 'Cannot my ways be understood?' Does he mean that God's ways can be understood at any moment by anybody, whatever he is like? You have just shown that it is not so. The Prophet himself supplies the answer:

'It is your ways that cannot be understood.' When we are remote from the ways God laid down for us, we cannot understand His ways. But in the end God always finds a way in which to lead us back to Him, and such a way that it is of our own free will that we turn to Him — and then we see that the very acts of God that seemed so strange were really part of His plan to save us.

"It will be so again — even if just now we cannot see it. After punishing us direly for our grievous sins, God has tested us with peace and prosperity. We seem to have failed, as you said — but who can tell? Perhaps the rot is on the surface only, perhaps there are many Jewish hearts like yours aching at this state of things, perhaps the nation is ready for another return to God more profound than any that went before . . ."

"But what will happen?" insisted the pupil.

"I cannot say what exactly will happen, or when. Something will happen though. — You are young, and things have been fairly steady in your time; even so you remember a Queen — the King's favourite wife — dropped suddenly on the word of a Minister . . . a Minister still in power, more so than ever — and you know his tendencies. — 'The laws of the Persians and Medes cannot be changed' says the Constitution — but policies can change, even constitutions can change, and dynasties and empires too . . .

"My father and those of his time were driven to this country in chain gangs by the Babylonians; the Babylonians have gone, but the Medes have no guarantee to continue forever, nor their policies . . . 'The heart of Kings is in the hand of God — wherever He pleases He directs it.'

"Don't be too sure of anything on earth. Of God you can be sure, that He will deal with us in His merciful way, which will be understood in the end. — But listen!"

A strange sound had come into the stillness. As it came nearer it resolved itself into the gallop of many horses. They listened with mounting fear. Most of the riders seemed to leave town by the King's highway, but groups split off; torches were lit, fanfares were blown in one after another of the town's quarters spread out below them. Finally, a small group of riders reached the market of the Jewish quarter just below them. They were soldiers, and Royal Messengers in their coloured livery. —

"Hear Ye All! Hear Ye All!" the messengers began, in Hebrew — for the constitution said that proclamations had to be made to each nation in its own language, and Jews now had equality. The market began to fill. A Royal Proclamation — but why at night time? What was the urgency?

"A law is proclaimed," they heard the messenger call out, "and inscribed in the statutes of the Persians and Medes which cannot be changed, that on the 13th day of the 12th month, that is the month of Adar, all Jews, men, women and children, shall be destroyed, killed and annihilated, and their property shall belong to whoever takes it." He went on with details: the frontiers were to be closed, anyone found sheltering Jews was to share their fate . . .

A stunned silence followed. The Rabbi tore his garments and sat on the ground.

It was some time before Shaltiel could marshal his thoughts. It was strange: His confusion had gone, and instead of deadly terror there was in his mind only one clear question. At last he dared to ask it of the Rabbi: "Is this what is to happen? Is it the end, my master?"

The Rabbi looked up. His face expressed sadness, but

his eyes looked clearly and steadfastly at his pupil: "It may be the end, my son; but it may be the beginning. — 'The heart of Kings is in the hand of God' — I see a sign of hope in this calamitous decree. If God had decided that there was no hope in us, He would not have given us a full eleven months before the destruction. I think that this is the test. If we are rotten to the core, we shall spend this time in useless attempts at bribery and political machinations, or each try to save his own skin with disregard for others, But if there is good left in us, we will turn to God, we will turn to Him with all our heart — and God is above kings and their laws."

Shaltiel was pondering over these words when he became aware of a new sound from afar, above the subdued murmurs from the market place. A wailing and crying, coming nearer, taken up by one voice after another. At last the procession reached the market place; at its head was an aged Rabbi, clad in sack-cloth. As he reached the torch light in the market place, Shaltiel recognised him: none other than "the Jewish Courtier", the famous Mordechai. And then he heard Mordechai speak to the Jews assembled in the market. The general wailing stopped as he began:

"This is from God! Our sins are great. Under the King's policy of peace and prosperity we have drifted away from our holy heritage. We have forgotten who we are, have become like others, have left the Torah. My brothers, Hear me! Let us proclaim a public fast for three days! Let us meet and consider our failings, let us repent and return to God! Let us beseech God to save us in our need, as He saved our fathers before us!"

Shaltiel expected that a few at least of the multitude would make some ugly interruption, for it was well known that it was Mordechai who had antagonised the Prime Minister by refusing to give him the honours ordained by the king. But no one interrupted, and general assent was given to Mordechai's demand for the fast.

As they went to join the meeting, the Rabbi said one more thing to Shaltiel:

"It is not the end, my son; it is the beginning!"

NO SLEEP THAT NIGHT

CHANANEL was walking with his father through the great market that formed the centre of the Jewish part of Susa. They had just tasted and bought a special jug of wine for the Seder. The merchant had put on a fresh clay seal, and Chananel's father had stamped it with his seal-ring. Now they were going to choose bitter herbs, and spices for the Charoseth.

The boy was excited. This was to be his first Pesach since he had become a Bar Mitzvah. Tonight he would be allowed to search for Chametz on his own in some rooms, and tomorrow he would keep the Fast of the Firstborn.

The market was full of Jews buying things for the Festival. It had been a good year, both for the farmers and the traders, and peace in the Empire. Everybody was in festive mood.

Suddenly, a silence spread through the market. They all stood listening.

From afar, from the direction of the Palace quarter, came a confused noise. The sellers hurried to pack up their wares. The strange noise was coming nearer. Now Chananel could see many people approaching along the main road from the Palace.

Now, one could hear frightened shouting and weeping.

Then, Chananel saw the man walking in front of the people. He had a sack wrapped round him. Under this he wore a long gown, like a Rabbi, but at the top it was torn to tatters.

Something terrible must have happened. Had someone died, an important person?

Suddenly, people nearby exclaimed "Mordechai!" and now Chananel, too, recognised the leader of the strange procession. Mordechai, the Sanhedrin's delegate at Court! Could this mean some danger at Court? That new Prime Minister, who called himself "Descendant of Agag, the last King of Amalek" — was he plotting against the Jews? But how could he, when the King had confirmed that all his peoples were to have equal rights?

The market had been cleared of merchandise, the people in it fell back as the newcomers crowded in. Then Mordechai mounted the overseer's platform in the middle, and in a tearful voice told them what had happened.

It was more frightful than anything they had feared. Not a tax on Jews, not an expulsion, not an anti-Jewish riot.

What Haman had plotted was the complete extermination of all Jews in the whole Empire — from Ethiopia to India — on one fixed day exactly 11 months later, on the 13th Adar.

The people cried out in anguish. Some tore their clothes, some were tearing at their hair. Mothers were pressing their children to themselves, as if the murderers were already upon them. Chananel himself was crying bitterly. For a time nothing was heard but the weeping of the people.

Then one man, dressed in rich clothes, made himself heard at last: "What is being done about it by our representatives?"

The cry was taken up. "Yes, what are you doing about it?" After all, one knew of proposed laws that had been rejected, after representation — and money in the right places. They waited for Mordechai to answer.

Mordechai spoke again. "Alas, my beloved brethren, you do not understand what happened. There was no draft proposal, no Council of Ministers. There was no warning sign at all until two hours ago, when Haman came out of the

Audience Chamber with the Decree, signed and stamped with the Royal Seal. It is now being copied and sent out with all haste. I have a copy here."

He read out some phrases: "To the Satraps, and the Governors of all provinces, to the Princes of all nationalities ... to exterminate, kill and destroy all Jews, young and old, children and women . . .their belongings to be plundered by the people ... a copy to be made law in each State, published to all nationalities, so they shall be prepared for that day.

"You know what the Royal Seal means by the Constitution of this country? It means that even the King himself cannot revoke this law. There is nothing that can be done, or could have been done, at Court."

"We can flee, or hide! " shouted one well-known merchant. "I shall share my money with 500 people, to help them escape, if others will do the same." A few men were heard calling out: "So will I! " "So will I! "

But again Mordechai dashed their hopes. "No, my brethern, this will help very little. Orders are being prepared to all border guards to prevent escape, and an order was issued already that anyone who hides a Jew, even his own slave, shall be put to death himself.

"No, my brothers, let us stop looking for loopholes. Let us see clearly for once. We are the people chosen to serve God, and show the holiness of His name to the whole world. But we have strayed from the true path, many times. The warnings of the Prophets did not help, the exile and the slavery did not change us. As soon as we were given equal rights, we started copying our captors. You all know that men from our richest and noblest families have shamelessly married heathen women. But they are not the only ones to blame. Ask yourselves, each of you: Are you proud of being God's people, or would you rather be a Persian, rich, strong, clean, perfumed — and drunk? Who did not drink at the King's Garden Party nine years ago? Who does not pay that idolatrous homage to this fiend from Amalek?

"We have no Prophets here, but more clearly than through a Prophet has God spoken through this bitter Decree. As Yonah told the Assyrians 'Yet forty days and Nineveh shall be overturned' — thus now we have been told 'Yet eleven months, and you shall be destroyed!'

"And as the Assyrians fasted and repented, so must we now fast and pray, leave our sins and resolve to keep God's commands. His mercy is infinite, and so is His power. He alone can save us, and to Him alone we must turn.

"Because of this, the Sanhedrin has ordered a three day's Fast, beginning tonight. One meal may be taken each evening, so the Seder can be kept as usual. It is true that one should not fast on Holy Days, but in this terrible danger we must not delay. May this fasting, when one should eat, atone for our eating in such places where we should have stayed away.

"We shall assemble here tomorrow before sunrise for special prayers. Go home now and prepare for the Fasts, and for the Festival. May He to whom all is possible change back our sorrow into joy, and redeem us as He did on these same days so long ago!"

It was strange, thought Chananel, as they waited whilst the people were leaving the market. A while ago they had been a terrified, shrieking mob, but now everyone was quiet. The people went away orderly, occupied with their thoughts.

Chananel, too, was thinking. Could it be that it was wrong to play with Armazd next door? Had he been too submissive to the heathen? Had he been learning too much of their Arts, and too little of God's Torah? Was it possible that such little sins could be the cause of this frightful, unimaginable punishment?

When they got home at last, Chananel saw Armazd standing in the street with his ball waiting for him. Chananel looked at him: a blond Mede boy, bigger and stronger than himself, less clever, but happier, more interested in fighting games . . .

Chananel had watched him torture a frog, and laughing. Was that because he did not know the true God? Might the same boy come into a Jewish house with a knife in eleven months' time?

When they came up to him, Chananel said: "I'm sorry, Armazd, I can't play tonight. We have a Festival tomorrow, and I must help prepare for it."

"Aw! " said Armazd, "Always your festivals! Can't they ever let you have some fun, like everybody else?" And he drifted off, looking for someone else to play with.

Chananel's father hadn't even heard them. He had gone on ahead, his head bowed, thinking. So he didn't notice the litter stopping next to Chananel. Armazd's father stepped out, and paid off the slaves. Chananel saw at once that he had been drinking.

"Hello, 'Ananel," the Mede greeted him, half-friendly, half-mocking. "What do you think of the news, clever one? You people have been nodding, with your famous influence at Court, eh? And what about your Invisible One? Let you down, hasn't He? Well, run and enjoy yourself while you may! I wish my stargazer could tell me exactly when *I* shall die, so I could use my time amusingly. Don't be afraid. There are still eleven months to go, so we are still friends. And when The Day comes, we won't stab you, it's much too messy. We'll just give you a little choke, like this —" and he tried to demonstrate it on Chananel's throat.

Chananel felt more revulsion than fright. In a flash he had lost all his respect for the heathen, grown-up or not. He pushed the man away, and said sharply: "Go away, Sir, go to bed; you have had too much wine. As for our God, don't mention His name lightly, or He might punish you swiftly. He is now punishing us for our sins, but don't say anything that you may regret. We shall change our ways and pray to Him, and if He wills, He can save us, as He saved Daniel and his friends, in spite of all the laws of the Persians and Medes. Good night! " And he turned away.

The man was still staring after him when he went into his house.

Now that it was over, Chananel was trembling. But now he knew that Mordechai was right. Mighty and "civilised" as these heathen were, they stood lower than the poorest Jews; without the fear of God one could not be a real man.

Later, as he went searching for Chametz, he thought: "Even if this should be our last Pesach it will be a real one. Already I feel the freedom, for I am not afraid of the heathen any more. And as we clear out the Chametz now, I hope we shall clear out all our sins, and become the people of God in truth. And then He *will* save us, even if He has to destroy the whole Empire first. Did He not do the same in Egypt, when we first became His servants?"

When the family assembled for supper, he saw that the same spirit was in them all. They feared God now, not Haman, so there was hope in the midst of their fear.

Next morning, Chananel got up early, and they went to the market. The place soon became crowded, and people who had come late were standing in all the surrounding streets. The Aron Hakodesh had been brought out from the Synagogue, dusted with ashes, as the people had dusted their heads. They prayed with contrite hearts, weeping aloud, and asking God to help them get free from sin. The Rabbi who acted as their Chazan, inserted special parts in the Tefillah.

Then the Sefer Torah was taken out, and the chapter about repentance was read and translated: "When you are oppressed .. and you will return to God, your God, and obey His voice — for a merciful God is God, your God — He will not leave you, and not destroy you . . ."

Then the oldest of the Rabbis spoke of their sins, and they wept, and promised from their hearts that they would change.

Afterwards, they went about the preparations for Pesach. At night they held the Seder, and Chananel's old grandfather told how God had freed their forefathers from Egypt. And they felt as if they had been there; for it was the same story. Oppression and danger, then the people crying out to God, and ceasing to be afraid of the masters and their idols — and then the miracles. And as they prayed that the redemption should be repeated, they were full of hope that it would be so this time, and they sang David's songs of thanksgiving, as if it were so already.

Thus passed the three days. Fasting and praying by day, and feasting and singing by night. It was strange, thought Chananel. They should have been desperate, but they were full of hope. At times the decree seemed to be only a bad dream.

The heathen, too, had stopped attacking them. They had begun to believe that these Jews were carrying on them, not the anger of the King, but that of the Invisible God.

On the third day a rumour went round that Esther had been received in the King's Throne Room. Many said "Ah, perhaps, the Queen can do something for us after all! " But the Rabbis reproved them: "Please, please, our brothers, do not look to human beings for help, for they cannot help. If help comes, it will come from God, in a way no man has expected." True enough, the outcome of that audience was something that no one had imagined — and that made them angry and ashamed: Whilst her brothers were fasting, the Queen had invited the King to a party — the King and Haman!

That made them realise that only God could help them, and they prayed with all their hearts.

That evening, towards the end of the third fast, Mordechai had called a special prayer meeting, for young boys only, in the Great Synagogue.

But when Chananel arrived, the Synagogue was already overfilled, and from where he stood he could not hear anything. He worried that he should have missed the most important meeting of all, and walked through the streets, disconsolate.

Suddenly he was startled by a noise of hammering and sawing. He found that he had wandered into the Nobles' quarter, and the noise was coming from the courtyard of Haman's Mansion. Dusk was falling, but the work was going on by flarelight. What could be so urgent that it had to be built through the night?

A group of labourers were unloading timber from a large ox waggon.

Chananel asked one of the men what was being built. "Special orders!" replied the workman. "The Prime Minister wants us to build a gallows, 50 cubits high, taller than any house, and it's got to be ready by morning. And you know who it is for? That rebellious Jew, Mordechai! And how do you like that, little Jew-boy?"

As soon as he could get clear from that street, Chananel started running. He had to get to the Great Synagogue and warn Mordechai.

But when he got there, panting, he found the place surrounded by armed guards, in Haman's private livery. No one was allowed in or out.

Chananel ran home and brought the terrible news. Mothers whose sons were there ran to the Synagogue, and their weeping could be heard all through the town.

Later Chananel heard that the mothers had obtained permission to send in food for the boys to break their fast but the boys had refused it. If they had to die, they preferred to die fasting. Chananel regretted even more that he was not there, for if anyone would go straight to Gan Eden, it would be his friends.

Everybody was stunned. So the blows were to fall already, and the first sacrifices were to be the purest. Mordechai their leader, and these innocent children!

No one slept that night. "Oh God, don't let this happen!" was the prayer on everyone's lips. They prayed as they had not prayed even in the last three days. The sound of the Jews' weeping rose from the whole town.

Morning came. Had God heard their last-minute prayers? People were trembling, waiting for a sign.

Then a strange thing happened. Through the streets moved a procession, a royal procession, with soldiers in colourful dress. Then came heralds calling out: "Thus is done to the man whom the King is pleased to honour!" After them came the King's own horse, led by a nobleman, and on it, in the King's Coronation Robes, rode — Mordechai!

And the man leading the horse was Haman!

What had happened? How had it happened? No one knew, no one could guess. But what it meant, the Jews felt in their hearts. God had heard them, His help was coming.

That evening, no one knew why, Haman was hanged — on his own gallows.

Next day one learned that Mordechai had been appointed Prime Minister in his place.

Within three months a new law had been passed — for a

law of the Persians and Medes cannot be revoked — giving the Jews permission to defend themselves on The Day, and making it the duty of the Satraps and Governors to equip and assist them.

The joy of the Jews was boundless. There were parties everywhere, singing and dancing in the streets. But in their joy they did not forget to whom they owed their thanks. Joyfully everyone promised again, that from now on he would keep every Commandment most strictly, and serve God gladly and with all his heart.

All this time Chananel had been much too busy and excited to think about Armazd. One evening the boy waylaid him as he was coming home from a class. "What is the matter, Chananel?" said Armazd. "Why don't you play with me anymore? Have you stopped being friends with me on account of what Haman wanted to do to you? I swear that I, and my father, and our whole family, had nothing to do with that. We were sorry for you, only there was nothing we could do. Don't hold it against us!"

Chananel looked at the boy's face. He saw fear in his eyes.

After a moment he answered "Don't worry, Armazd. We won't attack anyone. We don't lust for blood, or revenge. You see, we have the fear of God. But I just haven't got time to play with you any more. I have to catch up with the lessons."

THE RECRUIT

IT WAS with misgivings that Phidias saw Philodemos the philosopher crossing the courtyard towards him. Philodemos, though a Jew himself, was the strictest and most pedantically Hellenistic teacher of the Greek school at Jerusalem in which Phidias was a pupil, and the very sight of him always made him uncomfortable.

"Well, Phidias," said the teacher, "let me hear the poem you were to compose. I hope its hexameters do not shuffle along as abominably as you were doing just now!"

That was just like Philodemos; always reminding him of his ungracious way of moving and talking. Was it his fault that he had come to the school when he was already twelve? He had been sent there by his uncle after his father's death; until then he had been at a Jewish school and had been called Yosef.

Phidias had tried very hard to become a proper Greek, all these three years, for he admired Greek culture. But it was no good, he could not be like the others, and that was what he had been brooding on this last hour instead of doing his poem.

True, he was good in Geometry and Natural Philosophy, and his pronunciation and style were improving; but he was no good at the real culture subjects. He still felt horribly shy to go naked at the sports, and he still moved clumsily. "Here is one boy," the sports master used to say, "who will never run at Olympia" — and how they all laughed at that!

What would he not have given to be like the others! To

walk and talk like a real Greek, to be able to throw the discus as gracefully as the beautiful statue, a copy of the famous one by Myron of Athens himself, which stood in the gymnasium, and not, as the teacher said, "Like a Galilean shepherd throwing stones at his dog."

Or debating. His teachers, and the best boys, could turn out the most elegant arguments about any subject you set them, even about nonsense, but whenever Phidias spoke, the teacher said: "You sound like one of your old prophets, and what's worse, as if you had been translated at Alexandria. Can't you stop shouting from your throat and think of some logical argument instead?"

And they were right. He made a fool of himself every time he spoke, no matter how true his point was. To be sure, there were many boys who couldn't think of anything original to say, good or bad, but nobody reproved them as long as they were good at Gymnastics.

No, Phidias had thought, he would never excel at anything worthwhile. He would end up as a letter-writer, or with luck as an architect. Much as he would have liked to be a really cultured man, he was just not good enough. Then there was Religion. He was exempt from assisting at sacrifices, but he had to attend and watch, and that was really painful. Much of it was very beautiful to see, but he knew all the time that it was all wrong. These gods the Greeks believed in! They robbed and killed each other like the worst of men. Sometimes it made Phidias doubt if the Greeks were really as clever as he believed. Of course, he didn't say a word. Socrates had died for doubting the gods, and Socrates was a great philosopher even if one did not accept everything he had said. How would it look if a little Jew-boy were to try reforming the Greek Religion? Why, he would be killed like a dog!

All the same, why did they want the Jews to accept *everything* they did? Could one not have Greek learning, and yet keep to the religion of one's fathers?

Alas, he kept very little of his own religion. He prayed sometimes, but not properly; he had forgotten the words. If he had stayed among Jews, he would be wearing Tephillin now — the very pair his father had bought for him when he was still too young to wear them, and which his mother was keeping for him. He ate no pork if he could help it, and no meat at all if it could be managed. He had to write on Sabbath sometimes, but what could he do? He had to obey his uncle, hadn't he?

Of these things Phidias had been thinking, instead of the poem. Now he would have to find the best excuse he could . . .

"I beg your forgiveness, Sir," said Phidias, "but I have been unable to concentrate on the poem."

"Yes," remarked the teacher, with the enigmatic smile he so often affected, "I thought as much. Perhaps your thoughts were occupied with the incident at Modi'in? A fine mess your priests are getting into! Well, never mind; give me your opinion on it, as if you were speaking in the debating lesson."

Phidias had thought about the incident, though not just then. It was discussed everywhere and opinions differed from one extreme to the other; Phidias had considered them, and arrived at a balanced opinion.

What had actually happened was this: Some Greek priests, accompanied by soldiers, had come to the township of Modi'in to try to induce the population to sacrifice to Hermes. That was being done all over the country, on government orders, but in Modi'in there had been an incident. Matathia the Hasmonean, an aged and famous Cohen who lived in the town, seized a sword from a soldier and killed a certain Jew who had sacrificed. Then, lifting the gory weapon, he raised the ancient cry: "To me, whoever is for God!" Many local men had rallied to him and they had put the Syrians to flight. The rebels had taken to the mountains, and the government was collecting forces to hunt them down, but it was known that many Jews were joining the rebels and there might be resistance — though of course it could not possibly last long.

When Phidias had quickly gone over his points in his mind, he began, in his best style —

"In my opinion the rebellion at Modi'in must be deplored by every right-thinking person. Armed revolt against the rightful government can never be the correct and democratic way of settling a question. At the same time I must say that the local governors, or their executive officers, must bear a portion of the blame, for by their recent attitude of intolerance of Jewish beliefs, which is not in the highest tradition of Greek enlightenment, they have inflamed the feelings of the population. They should have been content to spread culture in the same quiet and peaceful way as our noble school, whilst respecting the religious feelings of the Jews. Or, if they wished to propagate the Greek religion, they should have done so in public speeches and philosophic argument, and not by force.

"Furthermore, I should like to observe that the rebels, deplorable though their action is, have shown a spirit of heroism and nobility which was thought to be dead amongst the Jews. By taking up a hopeless fight when nothing but ideas were at stake, they have followed in the steps of the old heroes of whom Greek poets sing.

"In this respect, the rebellion can be called a triumph of Hellenism, and I may conclude with the hope that when the wrongs of this unfortunate affair have been made good and forgotten, the stand of the few will be remembered as an example to inspire future generations of young Jews to deeds of fortitude and nobility."

The teacher's face had grown purple during this speech. He replied: —

"My dear Phidias, it seems that this school has taught you nothing at all. Either you are making a joke of a most serious thing or you are as impractical and illogical a Jewish dreamer as ever existed.

"To admit the action as wrong, and in the same breath to call it noble, nay, to compare it to the exalted exploits of Greek heroes, is the worst example of sophistry and blindness to truth I have heard for a long time.

"To accuse the King — for you know very well that the new policy was ordered by him — of intolerance, is the height of impertinence, apart from being rebellious. Are you suggesting that one should tolerate every local superstition that stands in the way of enlightenment, progress, and unity of the realm? Does your tribal law tolerate other religions? Did the Jews protest when all other tribes were induced to accept the truly universal religion of Greece, in which the philosopher and the washerwoman, the soldier and the merchant, can each find a god to his liking? Is not the need for force due solely to the stubbornness of the Jews alone amongst all the formerly barbaric tribes?

"Finally, how can you represent this ugly uprising as a protest against intolerance, when its first action was to slay a devout and innocent man, a Jew himself, whilst he was in the act of making sacrifice?

"No, my dear Phidias, I see that you are in a bad state indeed; in spite of what you say, you are more than half a rebel yourself. This is partly our fault; we have neglected our duty and pampered you, hoping that reason alone would be sufficient. I have watched you during sacrifices, and I know exactly what you think in secret. I shall put the matter before the teachers' council, and I will tell you now what I am going to advise: Tomorrow you shall officiate at sacrifice — or be handed over to the courts as a rebel and traitor.

"Do not come to classes this afternoon. Instead think and consider whether you are for or against us, so that tomorrow you shall be able to give us your decision in a clear and dignified way. Go now!"

* *
*

Phidias went, hardly knowing where he was going. He was shaken and frightened; he would have wept, but he had been taught that only women and cowards ever cried. What had he done to deserve this? He had only stated what he had believed — and still believed — to be the truth. Had not this very man taught him that one must tell the truth even at the cost of one's life? That one must listen to the opinions of others, even if they were wrong, without anger? That one must argue to the point and never about the person, and never take revenge on one's opponent for his honest opinion? Was it possible that these cool philosophers did not practise what they taught? That they were at heart as excitable, conceited and selfish as ignorant people? If so, why had he admired them all this time? No, it could not be true, or — or he had been wrong all the time, and the dirtiest village boy with his simple ideas was better than he.

And what was he to do now? How was he to reason things out if his life was threatened? Should he bow to force and pretend he had changed his views? But if so, how could he go on learning Philosophy if he really felt that his teachers were evil men who had forced him to live a life of untruths? Besides, he just could not do it. Sacrifice to Hermes? He had broken many laws, but he was still a Jew. He could not deny the true God.

Ought he to kill himself, as Socrates had done? No —

Socrates had been condemned by a court after defending himself bravely; he had known what he died for, he had not run away from a problem.

Run away? Was that what the teacher really wanted him to do? Was that why no one had prevented him from leaving the school — for, he had just noticed, he had wandered far away from the school buildings; he was now among the vineyards of the Kidron valley. But what was the point in running away! He would be caught in the end, if the government really wanted him, and then he would be called a coward as well as a traitor — and this time it would be true. No, he was no traitor, he was loyal to the king, and loved the Greek way of living — but why could they not leave religion alone?

* *

*

What was that? Something was rustling amongst the vines near the road. No one could be working in the vineyards this time of year — the grapes were far from ripe. A stray goat, perhaps? Phidias decided to look. He climbed over the stone fence and followed the sound. There was somebody there; Phidias saw him creeping through the vines: a boy about his own age, but dressed in Jewish garb, in the long tunic of a Yeshivah boy; and he wore tephillin. But why was he hiding? Phidias had nearly reached him when suddenly the boy turned round — pointing a dagger at Phidias. "Stand!" he ordered, in Greek, "or you die!"

"What is the matter?" exclaimed Phidias, in Hebrew. "Why are you threatening me? I only came to look."

"You are a Jew," said the other. "But you are dressed like a Greek." And raising his dagger he demanded: "To whom do you belong?"

"Belong?" wondered Phidias. "What do you mean? Are

you talking of the rebellion? But that is a local affair, far away! What are you doing in Jerusalem?"

"It is not a local rebellion any more!" replied the Yeshivah boy. "It is a holy war which all Israel has to fight. And I must know on which side you are, for I cannot let you betray me to the soldiers."

"Is that all?" said Phidias. "Well, I promise I will tell no one that I saw you. I swear it, by the God of Israel!"

"You swear by the God of Israel," said the boy, "but do you believe in Him? Are you on His side? You are a Hellenist, aren't you?"

"I believe in God!" declared Phidias. "Perhaps I shall have to give my life for Him tomorrow!" And he told the boy what had happened.

"And you are still hesitating?" asked the partisan. "You say you will not give way. Then why let them kill you, when it is your duty to kill them? Why don't you come away now and join us?"

"But what is the good of it all?" demanded Phidias. "How long do you think it can last? You are hiding in the mountains now. As soon as the army gets its reinforcements you will all be killed."

"Lord of the universe!" exclaimed the partisan. "Is that how a boy speaks who has once learnt of the Torah and the Prophets? Don't you know that God can help with many or few? Don't you remember Gideon, and Jonathan, and Chizkiyah?

"And if it be God's will that we die? Is it not our duty to die rather than bow to the idols?"

"But what do you hope to achieve?" asked Phidias. "Supposing you could throw the king's armies out of Judah. What do you want the country to look like? Do you want to give up all the things we have learnt from the Greeks all this time, and go back to a life of shepherds?"

"What does all that matter?" exploded the boy. "We can keep the crafts and sciences, they belong to anyone. But don't you see the real point? For a hundred years and more we have been taking the gifts of the Greeks and allowed ourselves to be deceived by their smooth tongues. We have become lazy in the wealth they have brought into the country, and — God forgive us — have treated His commandments lightly. You are only one of the Hellenizers, and not the worst of them. But all over the country Jewish children are growing up with the playthings of Athens, with arts and philosophies and sports and tales — and without knowing a word of Torah! And now they want us to worship their idols!

"You have seen that philosophy does not make a man good: your philosopher wants to kill you in honour of idols in which he probably does not believe himself — or if he does, the more foolish his philosophy. There is nothing in it, the whole lot of their fancy stuff. What matters is that they are heathens, and all they want in the world is to enjoy themselves — and be the masters of everybody else. We have the Torah, we and no-one else — and instead of teaching others something of the truth, we have been learning, bit by bit, to be like them!

"At last they have shown their true face. Where are their philosophy, their democracy and their morals, if they kill people, even women and children, who will not exchange the true God for naked marble figures? They are just as bad as any enemies of God have ever been, no, worse — because they do not want to kill our bodies but our souls!"

They were silent. How fiery, thought Phidias, and how brave and confident! And I, with my drill and sports, and my philosophy? I am supposed to be the noble one, the one who will die for truth!

Maybe he is right, and I have been playing with words

whilst the soul of my people is bleeding to death. Is that the spirit of Epaminondas — no, forget all that! Is that the spirit of a son of Judah?

He held out his hand and said: "Tell me where to go. From this moment I fight on your side — on God's side!"

And fight he did — from the ambush actions to the pitched battle in which the Syrian army was beaten, and on to Jerusalem where they drove the garrison from the Temple area. As he helped to pull down the idols that had been put there, he remembered how he had torn down the Greek lies within his own mind. As he learnt of the miracle of the lights, he knew that the light of the Torah would never be extinguished, but would one day illuminate the whole world.

START OF A WAR

> Rabbi Yochanan said: It is written (Proverbs 28): "Happy is the man who is always afraid (about what may come from his actions), but he who hardens his heart will fall into mischief." For because of Kamza and Bar Kamza Jerusalem was destroyed. *Gittin, 55b.*

THERE WAS A MAN in Jerusalem who had a friend called Kamza, and an enemy by name of Bar Kamza. One day this man gave a party and told his servant to invite his friend Kamza to it; but he went, by mistake, and called *Bar Kamza.* Bar Kamza thought that the other wished to make peace with him.

He found this very decent of him; for now that he considered the matter he found that he himself had contributed at least as much to their quarrels as the other. He made up his mind to greet the man as if nothing had ever happened; later he would take him aside and make a proper apology.

The day of the party came, and Bar Kamza went to his host's house, dressed in his best attire. Music greeted him in the brillianty lit reception hall; the room was filling with all the most important people in town. Bar Kamza exchanged greetings with those he knew. He noticed their surprise at seeing him there, but they must have drawn the same conclusion from the invitation as he had done. Indeed, his closer friends congratulated him on having made up the quarrel.

Suddenly the host of the evening joined the group. When he noticed Bar Kamza he stopped in astonishment. Then, reddening with anger, he said: "What are *you* doing here! Don't you know that I hate the sight of you?"

Bar Kamza grew pale. "But you invited me!" he began. "I thought..." He stopped, then went on: "There must have been some mistake. I'm sorry I came, but it wasn't my fault. But now that I'm here, please let me stay; don't shame me in front of everyone. If you like I'll pay for my meal..."

"No!" choked the other. "Go home! You are spoiling my evening."

Bar Kamza was angry himself now, but he controlled himself. "Please!" he pleaded; "Be reasonable. I'll pay half the cost of your party!" The other merely shook his head, shaking his clenched fists. "I'll pay for the whole party!" suggested Bar Kamza. "Only don't do this to me!"

The words sounded very loud; a hush had fallen on the room; everyone was looking at them.

The host came up to Bar Kamza, took him by the arm and pointed to the door.

Slowly Bar Kamza walked out. Surely all could see that the other man was behaving badly, surely someone would intervene, protest against this outrage!

But everyone stood still, looking the other way.

Hardly was he out of the door, when conversation and music started again.

Outside in the dark stood Bar Kamza looking at the lighted windows, choking with fury and disgust. How false they were, all these rich and honoured people, yes, and the learned men too! Not one of them had spoken up; not one of them had left the place of that ugly scene. Where was their piety, their learning? Was this the town called the home of Justice? By the Sanctuary, he would make them sorry for this! All of them, rich and poor, ignorant and learned — they were all alike!

* *

*

It was easy to make trouble just then. Judaea was a Roman Province, but there were many Senators who held that the Jews must be put down completely to make the country a safe base for the campaigns planned against Persia. The other inhabitants, Greeks, Idumeans and so on, could always be managed; but the Jews were wealthy and proud; they looked down upon the Romans as heathen and barbarians, and they were not even afraid of picking fights with the invincible Roman Army. Had they not rioted a year ago, when all that had happened was that one Roman soldier, probably after too many drinks, had insulted their Temple?

And from the reports of Governor Florus, it looked as if the Jews were on the point of rebellion. It was true, he was a tough one, this Florus; and even loyal friends of Rome had sent petitions for his removal, but if there had to be a showdown, then maybe it was best that he should go on provoking the Jews . . .

Now this Jew Bar Kamza had arrived, and was pestering everyone to listen to his "reliable information." He claimed that the Jews were in rebellion already, and preparing to attack.

He was given a hearing before a group of Senators. "The Jews of Jerusalem" he proclaimed, "regard themselves as independent of Rome, and treat the Emperor as an enemy!"

"How can you prove it?" asked the senior member of the Committee. "How do you propose to prove a thing that you admit exists only in the minds of your people?"

"I have a way of proving it," answered Bar Kamza. "Let the Emperor send an offering to the Temple. Let me travel with it, together with officers and men whom you can trust. I predict that the offering will be refused; they will not sacrifice it, for they are at war with Rome."

It was decided to make the test. A fatted calf was chosen.

A troop of soldiers was appointed to watch it and its keeper, and they and Bar Kamza sailed for Jaffa on a warship. They landed without mishap and set out for Jerusalem. The calf was carried on a wagon for, Bar Kamza insisted, it must not be tired and ill-looking, or the Jews would have an excuse to refuse it as unsuitable.

Indeed, he said, the offering and its escort must all look their best when they entered Jerusalem. So camp was made before entering, and the soldiers polished their equipment. "I shall wash and groom the offering myself," said Bar Kamza "It looks a little shaggy." He was allowed to do so, and he made it look very beautiful indeed — but he managed to make a tiny nick in one eyelid. This, he knew, was a blemish by the Torah, although the Romans would not call it one.

The news had been sent ahead, and the troop was joined by a detachment from the Jerusalem Garrison. They entered the city in festive procession. When they arrived at the Temple Gates, a delegation headed by the High Priest welcomed them. Speeches were exchanged, and the High Priest himself took the animal to the inner court. The soldiers — who, as gentiles, could not enter — were entertained in the outer court whilst preparations were made for the sacrifice.

The High Priest, however, did not go to the Hall set aside for offerings. He went straight to the "Hall of Square Stones," to ask the advice of the Sanhedrin, for he had noticed the blemish at once. He had sent Bar Kamza to wait in one of the Priests' Halls with a number of young priests to keep him company—and (as they had understood) to guard him well.

The rabbis saw at once that there was indeed a blemish, and that it had been made the same day, in just such a place where the Romans would not regard it as a blemish — and obviously by someone who knew the Law, by Bar Kamza himself. But what was to be done?

Unfortunately this was not just a question of law. One had to consider what the Romans would say — and the Jews. There had just been a furious dispute amongst the people about the whole question of accepting sacrifices from gentiles. This had always been done, and it was the law; but the War Party declared that it was an insult to the Temple to offer sacrifices for the benefit of the oppressors.

One Rabbi suggested that because of the danger from the Romans it was allowed to break the law and offer up the animal — to save the many lives that might be lost if this was not done. Most of the Rabbis tended to agree — but one, Rabbi Zecharyah ben Avkilas, whose piety they all respected, spoke against it: "Shall it be said that blemished animals are offered up on the Holy Altar?" For the moment no one had an answer.

The youngest of the Rabbis had got up to speak: "Let us exchange the animal for a good one. The soldiers will not notice it from where they will stand, outside the Gate."

"And Bar Kamza?" asked an elder Rabbi. "He will tell them!"

"Bar Kamza," answered the young Rabbi, "Bar Kamza is a traitor. He is trying to bring evil upon our people. It is the law that a man trying to kill another must be stopped, even if he has to be killed first. By that rule, Bar Kamza must not return to Rome alive!"

The Rabbis were pondering this suggestion, when Rabbi Zecharyah spoke again: "Will you have it said that a man was condemned to death merely for inflicting a blemish on a sacrifice?"

Before any decision could be arrived at the door was torn open. Bar Kamza was outside. He had insisted on keeping his eye on the calf, and the guards had brought him along.

Staying outside, where the Romans could see him, he demanded in a loud voice and speaking in Latin:

"What are you doing to the Emperor's offering?"

The High Priest answered him: "Peace, Bar Kamza; you are disturbing the deliberations of the Sanhedrin!"

"What is there to debate?" shouted the traitor. "Don't you know whether you are loyal to the Emperor or not?"

"Keep quiet please!" pleaded the High Priest. "The Rabbis must decide whether the calf is fit for sacrifice. It has a wound on an eyelid. We may have to wait till it heals up . . ."

"You are lying!" trumpeted Bar Kamza. "Anyone can see that this calf is the best that even the Emperor could have found; and you are insulting him by doubting it. I demand that you let me take it back before you do any harm to it!" And he strode in, and took hold of the calf.

Before anyone could stop him he was on his way back to the soldiers. Immediately they rode off — for Rome.

The War Party were jubilant: they had only been waiting for something like this. Anyone who spoke of explaining, or apologising, to the Romans was lucky if he survived the next night. The High Priest himself was killed by zealots.

It was war; and the longer Judaea held out against the legions, the clearer it became that all the attempts that were made to end the war were doomed to failure.

When the Roman's first expeditionary Army was routed, both sides became even more determined to fight to a finish. The Romans to save their prestige; the zealots because they had seen the Romans not-so-invincible.

Three years later the Temple lay in ruins.

THE LONG NET

IT WAS the first day of Pesach. In the Temple the Great Sanhedrin, the Supreme Court composed of the greatest Rabbis, was in session. On Shabbath and Yomtov there was no judging of court cases and they were in session only in case a question might arise concerning the sacrifices. Almost all of the 71 Rabbis were there, sitting in a semi-circle and discussing Torah questions. One of the members was giving his opinion on a point, when a Clerk of the Sanhedrin announced questioners. A Rabbi of the town was ushered in, followed by several men. The President of the Sanhedrin called upon the Rabbi to put his problem to the Court.

"My Masters!" began the Rabbi. "There is a problem here which seemed at first an unimportant quarrel; but if my suspicions are sound then this is something important and urgent enough to bring straight to you, My Masters, in your capacity of the Temple Authority.

"This man here" — he pointed to a middle-aged man dressed in costly garments of Persian style — "created a disturbance last night at the Seder by quarrelling with his landlord here" — he pointed to a portly man with flowing beard and payoth, dressed in the garb of Jerusalem's townsmen. "The quarrel was over what portion of the Korban Pesach the guest should receive, and these two witnesses" — he pointed out two Galilean villagers — "were members of the Seder company.

"This is not brought before you as a court case, My Masters, so I believe you will find it possible to consider it on

Yomtov. The curious point is that the man insisted on having the lamb's tail for his portion. When these people came to my house late in the night, I thought at first that I merely had to deal with an ignorant Babylonian who had never heard that the lamb's tail is one of the portions that are offered on the Altar.

"However, the man refused to accept my patient explanations and insisted that a great Rabbi had told him distinctly to insist upon tasting the tail. If he is telling the truth — and he insists on it — then there is a mystery here with which only you, My Masters, can deal."

All eyes had turned to the Babylonian, and the expressions of the Rabbis were grave. The President addressed the man: "Will you tell us your name and home town, please?"

"My name, Rabbenu," answered the foreigner, "is Ziggud bar Essur. I come from Arbela near the upper Tigris."

"And do you agree with what this Rabbi has told us?" asked the President.

"I do," answered the Babylonian, "and I am sure that the Court, the highest in the land, will grant me my right."

"Then tell us who told you to make your demand" said the President.

"No less an authority than Rabbi Yehuda ben Bethaira of Netzevin!"

A stir went round the court — how could that great Rabbi make such a suggestion? Was it not clear from the Torah that the tail had to be burnt on the Altar?

The President, however, showed no signs of perturbation. "And how," he asked, "did it come about that the Rabbi spoke to you about this?"

"When I was returning home from Jerusalem after Pesach last year, I passed through Netzevin, and stayed in the Rabbi's house for Shabbath. I told him how I had enjoyed the Pesach, how well my landlord had treated me, and how I had my choice of the lamb. Then he said, 'I am sure you were not allowed to choose just anything you liked; have you ever tasted the tail?' — and when I had to admit that I hadn't, he told me to be sure to ask for it this year — and so I did, only to have it refused."

The expressions on the faces of the Sages were varied; some signified disbelief, some doubt and others deep concentration. The President's smile was kind but inscrutable. "Tell us," he said, "how much Torah have you learnt?"

"Only very little, Rabbi. My father was poor, and I had to help him in business even before I was thirteen."

"But you learnt a little? Will you read to us a little from this Sefer Torah?"

The Babylonian was taken aback, but after a moment answered: "It was so long ago, My Master, I have quite forgotten how to read."

"Then will you recite the Shma' to us?"

The Babylonian began, but after the first sentence started to mumble. When asked to speak up, he grew very red in the face and said: "I must confess that I have not said it for many years; I am so busy, always travelling . . ."

"I understand," said the President, still smiling, and looked round the Court; by this time it was clear that his colleagues had understood too. He ordered the Court to be cleared. When only the Judges were left, a short consultation took place; then the strangers were recalled.

"Our decision," said the President, "is that this case shall be heard tomorrow. Meanwhile this man shall be safely lodged in the house of the Temple guard. We also order the Officer of the Mount to send his men in search of Jews from Arbela and the district who may be found in the town. They are to see this man for the purpose of identification. The

Levite Guards shall also arrange for a physical examination of their prisoner and report their findings tomorrow."

* *
*

One evening four weeks later, at Netzevin, the aged Rabbi Yehudah ben Bethaira was testing his pupils in the laws of Bikkurim, when a man came in and stood respectfully at the back of the Beth Hamidrash until the Rabbi called him.

"Rabbi," said the man, "I come to inform you, as you requested, of the arrival of the first group of returning pilgrims. Amongst them is a Rabbi from Pumbedetha, who has gone out of his way because he has a letter for you from the Sanhedrin. He asks me to tell you that he will be here shortly, as soon as he has stabled his donkey."

Rabbi Yehudah thanked the man, and told his pupils to repeat the tractate by themselves. He himself sat back and gave himself up to his thoughts.

A letter from the Sanhedrin! Could it be about the affair that had worried him all this year?

His mind went back to the incident almost exactly one year earlier.

* *
*

Spring had come late at Netzevin. Four weeks after Pesach the river that rushed down from the hills of Kurdistan was still swollen from the melting snow. Many travellers, returning from their pilgrimage to Jerusalem, had been held up in the town waiting for the water to subside. The Jews of Netzevin had been glad to put them up. They could not often manage the long journey to Jerusalem themselves, and indeed there was no duty for them to go since they lived outside Eretz Israel, but they respected all the more those who went, and were happy to help in their Mitzvah.

Rabbi Yehuda himself had a number of these travellers at his table on that Friday night. Most of them were Rabbis, some of whom had been his pupils, but one man from Arbela, an obviously prosperous merchant, had specifically asked to stay with the Rabbi. Rabbi Yehudah had taken him, particularly as the man had delivered a letter. Rabbi Yehudah often had correspondence with the Rabbis of the Holy Land, and usually the letters were carried by pilgrims.

As the evening progressed, the merchant, who had tasted quite an amount of the strong beer, grew more and more talkative, and the Rabbi, though he would have preferred to continue his learned discussion with the others, politely listened to what the man had to say. After all, Pesach in Jerusalem was something worth talking about, and the merchant told it well. He told of new buildings which Rabbi Yehudah himself had not seen when he was young enough to make the journey. He described the view of the Temple as one came in through the Eastern Gate; the rising terraces of the Inner Court, the great Altar on the left side — its gleaming white surface partly reddened from the blood of the many sacrifices being brought — and everything dwarfed by the majestic structure on the highest terrace — the Temple itself, more than ten times as tall as a house and at its front just as wide, its varicoloured marble sparkling like the waves of a sunlit sea. Through the open entrance of the Fore-Hall one saw the open doors of the Sanctuary itself. And over these doors — here a peculiar gleam had come into the speaker's eyes — the huge vine, made of solid gold, on which gold given for the Building Treasure — the "Bedek Habayith" — was stored in the shape of clusters of golden grapes and leaves. "I wish," the merchant had added, "they would leave me in there alone, for just one hour; there must be tons of gold in those grapes."

He had not noticed the scandalised looks from the people

around him, but taking another sip of his tankard, had gone on to describe Erev Pesach in the Temple.

"By noontime," he said, "you can't move. The Second Court, and even part of the 'Mount,' are packed with people leading their Pesach lambs. When the first group has gone in, the gates of the Inner Court are shut, but you can hear the Levites singing the Hallel as the sacrifices are brought. Then the people come out, carrying their lambs to be roasted, and another group comes in, and then yet a third!

"Such a lot of people! You know, the Kohanim can't even manage to carry the blood to be sprinkled on the Altar — they form chains, passing the golden or silver vessels to each other. And all these crowds of people are only one for each lamb! Each of them has his company waiting for him, and they get only a morsel each from the lamb, at the end of the Seder; of course, you have eaten a whole dinner before that, but that little piece of roast lamb tastes the best. And I always get the choicest part, you know; I am a wealthy man, and I pay well for my dinner."

The merchant stopped, and refilled his tankard from the jug. "Your beer is good, Rabbi," he said, "pity I couldn't drink any with the Pesach lamb, ha, ha!" Again his listeners looked shocked, but the man merely took another deep draught from his tankard. The beer was beginning to tell on him; he suddenly began to chuckle and then went on:

"But I haven't told you the best part of the story! You know how exclusive they are. Everyone must dip himself in the Mikveh, and before that be sprinkled with the purifying water on the third and the seventh day; and anyone who is not circumcised, or who does not believe in the Torah, must not take part at all. Well — little did my pious landlord dream that his favourite guest is a pure, hundred percent gentile! Ho, ha, ha . . ." He laughed aloud till he was quite out of breath.

The guests had jumped up with confused exclamations. Their eyes were on the Rabbi.

Rabbi Yehudah had motioned his guests to let him deal with the man. He had thought quickly. Here was a man who had committed a great crime, quite without compunction and with great daring. He must be familiar with Jewish laws and customs sufficiently to pass himself off as a Jew — after all, strange-looking Jews from many countries, speaking all sorts of languages, came up to Jerusalem; they could not examine everyone.

What could be done? To punish him here was impossible. This was not Eretz Israel; the government would intervene if a gentile was brought before a Jewish Court. To warn Jerusalem was useless — they would not be able to identify the desecrator amongst such crowds. No, the only thing to do was to lay a trap.

By the time the gentile had recovered from his laughing fit, Rabbi Yehudah's plan was ready.

"You are a daring man indeed," he addressed the gentile, in a half-admiring tone, "but I don't believe you have really eaten the very best part of the lamb."

"Sure, Rabbi! " the gentile had answered. "I was allowed to choose whatever part I liked."

"Ah," Rabbi Yehudah had said, "the best part of what was on the table. But did you ever get a chance to eat of the tail? You know the tail is the fattest, juiciest part of the lamb! "

"The tail?" the gentile had asked with a frown. "No, there never was a tail on the lamb when it came on the table. I wonder what happened to the tail . . ."

That was how it had ended — then. The gentile had moved on, and Rabbi Yehudah had not heard anything further. Had he taken the bait? Had he dared to go again, when he knew that some people knew his secret, people who might chance to meet him in Jerusalem? This was what Rabbi Yehudah had often thought about during the year. And now — what was in the letter?

The letter arrived soon: it was short, but long enough to gladden Rabbi Ychudah's heart:

"Peace to you, Rabbi Yehudah, who lives in Netzevin, but whose net is spread in Jerusalem,

from the Sanhedrin."

MY COW BROKE A LEG

THE AUTUMN SUN was peeping over a distant hill in Judaea that was still a self-governing province, though the sceptics said that Rome was only awaiting the end of her northern campaigns to crush her unruly vassal.

Up the road from the village walked a young man wearing the knee-long tunic of the peasant. The sturdy frame, the broad horny hands, were those of the peasant too; but the forehead was one made for thinking, and the mouth, though framed in a sparse black beard, was like that of a sensitive boy.

Eliezer was taking long strides. He would be late. His prayers must have taken him longer than he had thought. And his father had not wanted him to attend the synagogue at all today. They had so much work before them. The others would be finishing breakfast by now.

But he was glad he had gone. When he had fallen on his face at the end of his prayer he had asked for guidance, and now he felt in himself the strength of decision. Today he would tell his father that he must go. He had been put off too long. He must go to Jerusalem. As long as he could not study, his life would be worthless. Here he was, sowing and cutting, threshing and ploughing, caught in the wheel of the farmer's life, and all the time he was yearning for enlightenment and understanding. The few lessons that the local teacher gave them only showed him how much there remained to be learnt, how much there remained to be understood even in what the teacher had dealt with. When would he learn it all?

He was over twenty already, and he had a suspicion that Hyrkanos, his father, would never let him go. No, he had come to the end of his patience. After sowing-time he would go. He would tell his father today. Let his brothers do his share as well; they had no wish to study.

He could not see anybody about the farm house. Ah, there was his father bending over a sack of grain. He went up to him and greeted him. "How late you are, Eliezer!" was the reply. "Your brothers have eaten their bread and gone to the fields, and so have the hired men, but you — you must go to the Beth Hamidrash and stay for an hour, as if you were the only God-fearing man here. Have you forgotten the ploughing? We have delayed too long already. The second rains may be on us before we have sown, God forbid! We must finish it all today, and it's the Eve of Shabbath!"

"My father, I must speak to you," said Eliezer. "I cannot stay here any longer. After the sowing, I must go before Rabban Yochanan ben Zakkai and . . ."

"Take care, boy, how you speak to your father! Are you not a farmer's son? Here is the ploughing to be done, and you speak of your dreams? I tell you that I cannot spare you. Look at those fat acres! They were poor and stony when I bought them. And now that I am getting old they will return to waste and ruin if you do not take care of them. I have risen to prosperity, thank God; but only through my own hard work. What would you be if I had stayed in Jerusalem? A homeless beggar! Let those study who have slaves to do their work, or the priests who collect their gifts anyway!

"Don't stand there looking at me! Take your ox and your plough and get to work — before you raise my anger! You will eat when you have done your work."

Without a word Eliezer went to the stable. Of course they had to leave the oldest ox for him. And he had seen them in the level fields. The hillside they left to the youngest brother and to this decrepit beast. Well, it did not matter. Nothing mattered.

He had come with such firm resolve — and a few words had silenced him!

Well, there was ample time for thinking in the field. He lashed the plough on to the ox's back and led it out. He must hurry if he was to complete his work and be back in time to wash himself before sunset.

He arrived and harnessed the ox to the plough. He began to work. His father might have cleared many stones away, but here, at any rate, he had left enough for him. And there in front was an outcrop of rock. Careful now, lift the plough a little! The soil is shallow here. What would his father say if he returned in mid-day with a broken ploughshare? All-right — he was past the danger-spot now.

How was one to live in two worlds at once? Now it was his father urging him to work; before long he would have the responsibility for a family. How was a man to find time for studying the Torah? If only he had already acquired some fundamental knowledge! He might then repeat it, follow up lines of thought, even whilst working — though on a field like this, he needed all his wits for the work.

What was the good of being the son of a wealthy farmer, if it only meant more work? Far better to be like his friend Chananyah, whose father had a few acres on the north side of the hill. Chananyah had been at Yeshivah these three years; he would be a learned man one day. What did it matter that he was considered a poor man compared with Eliezer's family? Eliezer himself would gladly give up his rights in this farm for his freedom. But he was chained by his duties to his father. Was it right that his life should be marred out of respect to his father's wishes?

Hoi, what was that? What business had the ox to fall down? The field was not as difficult as that! This ox should have been killed long ago; it was simply not fit to be working.

He went up to the ox, helped it to rise. No use: it rolled over on its side. And now he could see that it would never rise again: the left knee was dislocated, broken maybe. A nice business!

A few hundred cubits down the hillside, he could see his eldest brother. He shouted to him, and he looked round. "Broke a leg! Leg... Broken!!" shouted Eliezer, pointing to the stricken beast. The other stopped and tethered his ox; he was coming up.

What now? Eliezer had a vivid vision of his father imposing punishment. How could he help the ox being so clumsy? And if he was a bad ploughman, why did they give him the worst animal for a hillside field?

The next thing he knew, he was fleeing uphill. He could hear his brother shouting: "Where are you going?" But he did not stop. Where was he going? Away from here, away from their reproaches! But whereto?

An old saying was humming in his head: "It was for my good that my cow broke a leg."

He reached the hilltop, the rock and the heather. He felt safer here. Many a time in his boyhood had this been his retreat, when trouble was afoot, or when he felt that he just had to be alone. From here you could not see the farm. You only saw hilltops; when the weather was clear you could look out to the sea in the west, and in the east you could see the higher ranges where Jerusalem lay. Jerusalem! How he yearned for Jerusalem!

Why not? "For my good the cow broke a leg!" Why not go to Jerusalem? This was his opportunity for going without defying his father openly. He would think he was just hiding from his wrath. Then, from Jerusalem, he would let him know. It was easy.

He would go on across the hills and come down to the Jerusalem road. Then he would walk on and on until he could sit down in Rabbi Yochanan's hall of teaching. It was only just over a day's journey to Jerusalem.

Sunset found him in the shelter of a wine press hewn in the rock, above the Jerusalem road. He had had no food all day, except some half-rotten vegetables left in a field, which he had choked down with a feeling of nausea. It was windy up here, but his forced march across the hills had tired him, and he went to sleep on the stone floor.

He awoke early, frozen and stiff. He walked around to warm himself, but could not continue his march beyond the 2000 cubits on Shabbath. He sat down in front of his cave, musing. He thought of what his people were thinking. It did not seem so simple now. With the dull gnawing in his stomach, and stripped vines and bare fields in front of him, he did not feel the ease and the cheer that the Shabbath demanded, but there was a new serenity as he repeated to himself: "I am going to Jerusalem; at last I am going to sit at Rabbi Yochanan's feet."

With nightfall he descended to the road and made up for the enforced rest by walking throughout the night. Twice he was challenged by Roman soldiers, but he explained that he had taken a vow to visit the Temple, and they let him go on after searching him.

* * *

Weak and tired, Eliezer reached Jerusalem the next afternoon. In the study hall he introduced himself as a new student from the country. An older student offered him a lodging in his house; there was a spare divan in the living room. He accepted, but he let it be understood that he had already arranged for his food. He could not bring himself to eat the bread of charity.

Instead he would steal out in the evenings, when the markets were being swept, and compete with the beggars for abandoned fruit. He was not always successful, and what he got was accepted ungraciously by a peasant's stomach.

But this worried him less than his studies. He just could not follow the lectures. There were so many details, so many references to unknown things. Inferences were made by rules that puzzled him. What he could glean were unconnected fragments. Oh, for the years he had missed!

Was he really too old to begin, as his father used to say?

His father! He had disobeyed him, hoping to justify it by his attainments in the Law. Where were his attainments now! He would never get anywhere like this.

He sought out a priest of their acquaintance, who had come up for his week of temple duties, and asked him to speak to his father for him. He never had an answer.

When his father came up for Passover, Eliezer went to see him. He was not admitted.

It hurt Eliezer to remain in disgrace, to be refused a chance of asking forgiveness; but he would not surrender.

He threw himself into his studies, begging right and left for coaching, sitting up late.

His health suffered. One day, in the middle of a lecture, a student nudged him and said he had been told by the master to find the man whose bad breath was causing a nuisance, and ask him to leave. Eliezer got up and went away weeping.

The Rabbi had him recalled, and asked: "Why are you crying?"

"Because I am being cast out from the study hall as if I were a leper!" Eliezer brought out.

The old sage searched long in the emaciated face, in the

glowing eyes of this youth who was holding on to his work with his last strength. Then he spoke:

"Indeed, as this bad odour is now coming from your mouth, so one day the scent of Torah will proceed from your mouth from end to end of the world."

Eliezer was dazed. Had he heard alright? Had the master said that, or was it a hallucination? Could it be true that he, who did not understand what the scholars were saying, would become a teacher in Israel?

But the Rabbi had not finished. A mysterious smile was playing on his lips as he said: "Tell me, what is your father's name? I cannot recall it."

He had asked him before, but Eliezer had purposely hidden the name in a mumble. Now he would have to tell him; what would the Rabbi say? Would he tell him to go home and recuperate? Or would he ask how the son of a landowner came to be poor?

But when he had told him, the Rabbi replied, still with that unfathomable smile: "Hyrkanos of K'far Zecharyah? Why, I know him well! You are the son of such an important man, and I did not know! In future you must eat at my table!"

He had not the strength to decline the invitation. For weeks, during the meals in the Rabbi's house, he awaited and dreaded the questions that must come. But they were never asked.

The master's prophecy (had it really been spoken?) gave him energy, and his health returned with regular meals. But now there was something between him and his friends, an unspoken question: Was it fitting for a sage to prefer a man because his father was wealthy?

Had they only asked it! He could have told them to what his preference amounted. He was out of place at that table. The master hardly noticed him, and he sat among chosen scholars whose every word or movement showed him how desperately far he was from their level. Never had he felt more lonely.

His longing for his family returned. Was he cut off from them forever?

He took refuge in the depth of the Law. Years passed.

Came a day of celebration in Rabbi Yochanan's hall. A cycle of study had been completed, and the Rabbi might use the occasion to lay his hand on some of the older scholars and pronounce them Rabbis. Never had the hall been so crowded. Every notable in the city had come; former students flocked to their master.

The Rabbi's lecture began with a summary of some of the teaching of the past months, but in a festive mood he soon went on to ethical precepts and thence to tales of great men of the past.

During a pause an innkeeper pressed up to him and delivered a message. The Rabbi told a student to go with the man and watch for the arrival of Hyrkanos from Kfar Zecharyah whom he was to conduct to a place of honour.

*

* *

Hyrkanos was confused by the unsual crowd. Meekly he followed his guide. What was going on here today? He might have to wait all day before someone would deal with his business.

Where had they put him? These were not students; and they could not all be litigants! He could recognise some public men. Was not that Nakdimon ben Gurion, the man who in the drought four years ago had bought from the Government all the water needed for holiday crowds at a fabulous sum? He had never been near him before. And the young man over there was Ben Tzitzith-ha-Kesath, who never trod on bare ground except in the temple court. He felt small in such company. And his neighbour . . . he trembled: that was Kalba Sabua, who had enough grain and oil in his storehouses to feed Jerusalem for years!

The end of the lecture roused him from his musings. Would the crowds go now? Could he bring up his case soon? No, it seemed there was more to come.

A young man was brought to the Rabbi. He seemed to be resisting some request. Hyrkanos could hear his exclamation: "But I am not able! " A murmur went through the hall.

Now the man had given way. He turned round and faced the audience. There was silence, the tension of expectancy. He began a discourse. Did he not look like Eliezer? Even the voice was like his. But what an idea! This man must be an advanced scholar if he was addressing the meeting. And Eliezer — he had made enquiries about him, but even people connected with Rabbi Yochanan's circle did not know his name. The innkeeper who knew him of old had only seen him once, and then — he shuddered — he had seen him picking up rotten food in the market place . . . A vagabond! What had he done to deserve this disgrace?

The young speaker had got into his stride after a bashful start.

A tension had gripped the audience. There were half-loud exclamations here and there. Someone behind Hyrkanos said: "From where does he get that? Have you ever heard it?" Another answered: "No. But he has proved it clearly enough, hasn't he?" And the first: "Maybe, but what authority . . ." "Sh! ", interrupted the second voice, "look at the Rabbi! "

The Rabbi had risen. He embraced the young man and exclaimed: "This is correct! It is the truth! You have instructed me, Rabbi Eliezer! "

Rabbi Eliezer? Could it be his son? But "Rabbi"! Hyrkanos jerked round and asked one of those who had been discussing the speaker: "Who is he to whom the Rabbi said this?"

The other put a finger to his lips: the speaker was beginning again. When he saw he could not shake him off, he said: "That is Eliezer ben . . . ben Hyrkanos."

Hyrkanos jumped up and started at the speaker. His son? How could that be? But it was true; he recognised him now beyond doubt. But how did he come to be up there? Had everybody been lying to him?

"Sit down!" hissed somebody behind him. His neighbours were turning towards him.

Now Eliezer looked his way. Ah, he had recognised him. He had given a start. He stopped speaking, then began again and wound up his discourse. He was being congratulated by his friends. But he was trying to get rid of them, and was making his way towards Hyrkanos.

"Oh, father!" he cried as he reached him, "how happy you have made me by coming! Have you really forgiven me?"

Hyrkanos found it difficult to speak. "Yes, yes, my boy," he brought out at last, "all is well." And he was patting Eliezer's shoulder as he spoke.

Suddenly Eliezer asked: "But how did you know the master was going to call me? I had no idea myself! Did he let you know beforehand?"

Hyrkanos felt hot as he answered: "N-no, my boy, I did not know either. To tell the truth, I did not come to hear lectures. I came to get a court to disinherit you. You see . . ."

He suddenly became aware of the people who had collected around them and quickly went on:

"But instead, my dear son, you shall be made my sole heir!"

Why did the bystanders seem so embarrassed? Someone had even coughed out a laugh.

But Eliezer did not seem to notice. He said:

"You are very good to me, my father. But we must not rob my brothers. Your peace is the greatest gift you can make me. And if God desires me to be rich, does it not say. 'Mine is the silver and the gold'?"

THEY CALLED HIM A TRAITOR

THROUGH THE TALL, NARROW WINDOWS the moon shone on a tastefully furnished room. The lamps on their brass stands were unlit, though the room was occupied. Three men sat on damask-covered couches around a low table, on which lay an open scroll. Another man was leaning against the wall near the heavily barred door. Their languid attitudes made them appear old and tired, and their faces were emaciated, but their sparse black beards showed that they were still young, and the occasional eagerness that came into their low-voiced discussion proved that their spirit was not broken.

They wore the long white gowns of Torah scholars, but over these they had belted heavy swords, and other weapons were leaning against the walls. In besieged Jerusalem, torn by internal strife, even Rabbis had to be ready for self-defense.

Suddenly, at a signal from the guard at the door, they fell silent and listened tensely. Slow, cautious footsteps were approaching. Then came a tapping at the door. The man on guard went to a window and whispered through it: "Who is there?" The others drew their swords and took up positions near the door.

A whispered answer came from the outside: "Let me in; I must speak to the Rabbi."

"Who are you," repeated the guard, "and why do you come at night?"

"My business is urgent and secret," answered the man outside. "I cannot tell you my name, but tell Rabbi Yochanan ben Zakkai that the boy whom he used to carry to the Beth Hamidrash is outside."

"Wait, then," answered the guard. He went to a door leading from the room and knocked. When a grey-haired Rabbi opened the door, he said: "Rabbi Eliezer, will you tell our Master that a stranger wants to see him urgently. He describes himself as the boy whom the Rabbi used to carry to the Beth Hamidrash."

Rabbi Eliezer replied: "The Rabbi sent for him. Let him in, carefully, and let no one ever speak of this visit."

One man, his sword raised, posted himself next to the door whilst another unbarred it and opened it half way.

A tall broad-shouldered man came in. His face was hidden in his dark cloak, but his bearing was that of a military man. The door was barred again. The stranger surrendered a dagger, and submitted to a search for hidden weapons. Rabbi Eliezer conducted him into the inner room.

He struck a flint and after a few moments had lit one of the lamps. Its light revealed a white-bearded Rabbi reclining on one of the couches. His body was shrivelled, but his face, now showing an expression of deep seriousness, was neither old nor young; it seemed to be beyond age, to shine with an inner light.

Rabbi Eliezer left them. Rabbi Yochanan motioned the stranger to a seat, but he remained standing, towering above him. He removed his cloak, revealing himself as Abba Sikra, the commander of the zealots.

"Peace, Abba Sikra," said the Rabbi, "and I wish it were really peace..."

"It is a just war we are fighting," declared the commander, "a war for our freedom!"

The Rabbi answered quietly: "It is a war that should have been avoided. In time Rome would have replaced

Governor Florus. And whatever we suffered from him is as nothing compared with what we are suffering now. As for the future . . ."

Abba Sikra drew himself up. "Is it my fault that the storehouses caught fire? If we had them we could laugh at the enemy."

Rabbi Yochanan looked at him steadily. Abba Sikra dropped his eyes. He knew well enough whose fault it was, and that those responsible were still under his command.

The Rabbi went on: "Meanwhile thousands are dying from hunger. Do you still expect to win?"

A note of triumph came into the commander's voice as he retorted: "Is that a way for the Head of the Sanhedrin to speak? Does it not say 'Nothing prevents God from helping, with many or with few'?"

"Nothing does, if He sees fit to help." replied the Rabbi, unruffled. "But is it a just war? When this war started we had not been attacked, nor was there an attempt to prevent us from keeping the Torah. Your party calls it a war of liberation.

"What do your friends mean by liberty? Freedom to worship God, or power and worldly honours? As for the people, they are not even fighting for that. They were incited by your party's slogans, against the counsel of the Rabbis, and now they are only kept in the city by sheer terror. They would not give their lives for Independence. They have existed under Rome for more than 100 years and so have stronger countries. Greece and Egypt, Gaul and Britain— none of them make a fight for independence now.

"No, you know it is not reliance on God that keeps your friends in the fight. It is obstinacy, or fear of the Romans' punishment. I asked you: do you, by your earthly way of thinking, really expect to drive off these crack legions with your untrained, starved men?"

The Commander did not answer.

"It is still not too late," continued the Rabbi. "Vespasian is still calling on us to surrender and promising to spare the city and the Temple. It is true he will now impose punishment, but it will be little compared to what he will do if we hold out. You always talk of dying for the people. What is better in a hopeless situation: that the leaders of the rebellion should risk execution and the people live — or that, God forbid, all should perish?"

Abba Sikra sat down and hung his head. After a full minute he said tonelessly: "It's no use. If I suggest surrender now, my own men will kill me as a traitor. It has gone too far. God help us."

There was silence.

A chill hung over the room; in the distance one heard a woman weeping. It seemed as if Zion was bewailing her sons.

Thus they sat. The woe of all the ages was on them. The long, the bitter Galuth was descending on the Sons of Israel.

They were silent for a long while. Then the Rabbi raised himself, his expression one of unutterable sadness, his eyes looking into the distance. He was speaking in a low voice, as if speaking to himself. "It has come then. The prophecies are being fulfilled. The Destruction, The Slavery. The terrible long wandering. The age of darkness. The martyrdom of the body, the martyrdom of the soul. The poor scattered flock, the poor beloved children of our people . . ." He wept quietly.

After a time he began again in a firmer voice: "The remnant shall return; that too is prophesied. The Torah will not be forgotten; that too is said. When Rome has fallen, and Athens been forgotten, we shall still be the witnesses of God!"

Abba Sikra could not understand it. The man was sad, sad unto death, yet a strength was welling up in his words. His own despair gave way to a strange feeling of hope. It seemed mad, yet he felt that this mad hopefulness was a thousand times more sane than the obstinate determination in his own camp. He suddenly saw that the Rabbis had not been traitors, nor had they been blind to the sufferings that had stung him into fighting. If only they could have marched together . . .

In a new, strong voice the Rabbi was saying: "This is a time for action, not for talk. And you must help me. I must go to Vespasian. Command your men to let me go!"

"But he will kill you!" cried Abba Sikra. Then he remembered that the Rabbi was on the black list of the Sikarin, the dread secret society, at this moment, that his own military court would have condemned him as a "friend of the Romans" if they had not feared the population, and he hung his head.

Rabbi Yochanan smiled. "But what is death in a great cause?" he said, his intonation suggesting the oft-repeated slogan of the zealots.

"What do you expect to achieve?" asked Abba Sikra. "Do you think he will call off a war of the People and Senate of Rome on the prayer of one man?"

"Alas," said the Rabbi, "I would give my life a hundred times if I could achieve that. But perhaps he will spare the sages and their disciples. And if the root survives, the tree will grow again."

"I don't think you will even see him," replied Abba Sikra. "The Romans will arrest you as soon as you come out, and crucify you like those." He pointed, as if he could show the Rabbi the bodies of the deserters hanging from hundreds of crosses on the hills around the city.

"Besides," he continued, "my guards will never allow you to leave. I can't make exceptions, least of all with a man like you. No one passes out of this city alive." He was silent for a moment.

"No one alive . . ." he repeated in deep thought. Then he bent forward and began to whisper to the Rabbi.

Half an hour later he left, and the Rabbi had a whispered conversation with his disciple Rabbi Eliezer.

In the morning Rabbi Eliezer informed the others that the Rabbi was in pain. The news spread quickly. There was a rumour that he had the plague. All day people were crowding in front of the house. Only pupils and friends were allowed to see the Rabbi, from the door of his room. All over the town people forgot their own desperate position and prayed for the Rabbi's recovery.

The next morning no one was admitted. "The Rabbi is still asleep," was the answer to all callers. But the rumours were spreading.

About noon the noise of hammering was heard in the house. This confirmed the rumours. The crowd wept and moaned. A voice cried out: "Rabbi, why have you left us behind?" The cry was taken up: "What will become of us?"

Then Rabbi Eliezer appeared in the doorway, his garment torn. He held up his hand for silence, then he proclaimed:

"Rabbi Yochanan ben Zakkai has asked for the following things:

"He shall be taken out of the City without delay. No mourning meetings shall be held.

"No one but Rabbi Yehoshua and myself shall carry the coffin or even approach it. Other pupils will form a square round the coffin at a distance of four cubits, to ensure that no one approaches.

"His bed and all other articles in his room shall be burned; the Holy Scrolls shall be buried. The room shall then be locked. The pupils who have stayed in his house shall remain there for thirty days.

"I ask you to obey his wishes, and now to clear a space in front of the house."

A murmur went through the crowd: "The plague!" Soon there was a clear space in front of the house.

The coffin was carried by the two Rabbis: Eliezer and Yehoshua. Around it walked a group of other pupils; in front and behind went the weeping crowds.

The sun was setting when they reached the Water Gate, on the South-east of the city. Slowly the coffin came to the front. The guards stopped them. "Where are you going?" demanded the sergeant on duty.

"To bury Rabbi Yochanan Ben Zakkai," replied Rabbi Eliezer. "You know that by the law a dead body must not be kept overnight in Jerusalem."

The sergeant consulted his captain: "How do we know he is really dead? Shall I pierce the coffin with a javelin?" They went on conferring. The crowd began to murmur.

Suddenly there were salutes. Abba Sikra had appeared on the scene. The problem was submitted to him.

"No," he said. "We cannot do that. This crowd will get out of hand if we stab their beloved Rabbi."

"Let us shake the coffin then, and see if he moves," suggested the captain.

"No," said the Commander, "any kind of disrespect will provoke a riot. They will say that we feared him in life, and took revenge on his dead body. It is likely enough that he is dead. He was old and weak; younger people have succumbed."

He turned to the two Rabbis. "You will be sent out as soon as it is dark. Keep in the shadow of the wall as long as possible, and make no noise. If the enemy spots you, surrender or flee, but don't lead them here. If you should come back safely, come to this gate and give this special password." He whispered to them: "Resurrection."

When dusk had merged into darkness, and the sentries on the gate tower had reported a clear field, the gate was opened a fraction, the two Rabbis passed through, and it was barred again behind them.

They went in the direction of the family vaults, but as soon as they were invisible from the wall, they changed course. They went down into the Kidron Valley and made for the Roman lines.

Soon they were challenged by the outposts. They surrendered quietly, and upon their demand were led to the Centurion's tent, still carrying the coffin.

The officer came out to look at them by torchlight. He was still holding the goblet from which he had been drinking.

"Well, well!" he joked, "the Jews are learning what to expect. Now they come dressed in their shrouds and bring their coffins. But we need two coffins, my little Jews. Or are you thin enough already to go in together?"

"Sir," replied Rabbi Eliezer, respectfully but without fear, "we come to announce the surrender of Rabbi Yochanan ben Zakkai. The Rabbi humbly begs an audience with the General."

"Ah," said the officer, "that is different. John Zaccaeus! We have reports of him. Leader of the Synhedrion and a friend of Rome. Wants to negotiate, I suppose. I'll see what I can do. Where is he now?"

"The Rabbi is here with us," said Rabbi Eliezer, making a move towards the coffin.

The officer was speechless for a second. Then he erupted: "Are you still mocking us, confounded rebels? Surrendering after he is dead! We will torture you for this!"

"Sir!" replied Rabbi Eliezer. "Rabbi Yochanan is alive. With your permission I shall open the coffin."

Understanding dawned on the Centurion. He burst out laughing: "Ha ha! so that's the answer to the riddle! The joke is on the Jews this time! Capital, capital! The Trojan horse in reverse! Bring him out, bring him out! I must report this at once! The General likes a good story at the banquet."

The Rabbis opened the coffin and helped Rabbi Yochanan out. He was a little out of breath, but otherwise unharmed. He bowed to the officer and said simply: "Sir, I am in your hands."

The captives were escorted to the general's pavilion, the Centurion hurrying ahead.

Vespasian was feasting with his friends and staff officers in front of his pavilion. He was still laughing at the officer's story when the captives were brought up. He ordered Rabbi Yochanan to be brought to him at once.

The Rabbi bowed low, then proclaimed: "Peace unto you, O Emperor!"

Vespasian was taken aback, but after a moment he answered sternly: "You have doubly incurred the death penalty. Once for addressing me as Emperor when you know well that I am not the Emperor, and again for remaining with the rebels and not surrendering until now."

Rabbi Yochanan did not flinch, "Indeed and indeed," he repeated, "you are the Emperor. Our prophets have said that the Temple will fall into the hands of a ruler. Since the city is about to fall, you must be the Emperor. As for my not surrendering before, I wish I could have come before, not only to surrender myself but to bring you the surrender of the City and end this tragic war. But the zealots amongst us have seized power, and prevent anyone from leaving the town. They will not let us surrender."

Vespasian, visibly flattered but unwilling to show it, answered incisively, in the manner of a public orator: "As for the first, it only proves that your prophets can be wrong. As for the second, it is no excuse. If a snake is coiled round a jug of honey we must kill the snake though we break the jug. If you can't control your brigands you must suffer for them."

Before Rabbi Yochanan could think of a retort, there was a commotion. Trumpets were blown, a troop of horses were heard racing through the Camp. In a moment they arrived. A dust-covered officer jumped off his foaming horse and came up to Vespasian, handing him a despatch. Without waiting for him to read it he turned to the assembly and called out: Vespasian has been proclaimed Emperor. Long live Emperor Vespasian! "

All joined in the shout, and it was quite a time before Vespasian remembered his prisoner. When he addressed him again it was with some awe: "Your prophets were right after all! I can't understand how a people with such wisdom should get into such foolish mischief. But since you have augured well for me your life shall be spared."

On an impulse he said: "Ask me a favour before I depart for Rome," then added with a twinkle in his eye: "But don't make it too big, you know, or you will get nothing."

Rabbi Yochanan answered gravely: "Your majesty, I have three things to ask, small to you, but dear to my heart. Firstly, give me the town of Jamnia, or Yavneh as we call it, and let me build a college there, where the remnant of our sages shall study and pray. Secondly, spare the family of our religious leader, our Nasi; they had no share in the rebellion. Thirdly, grant me doctors for my friend Rabbi Zadok, who for the past 40 years has been fasting and praying that this catastrophe should be averted; now he is unable to take solid food. These are the favours I ask. May it please your Majesty to grant them."

"Is that all?" asked the Emperor in high spirits. "I thought you would never stop. You are a proper Phoenician for bargaining. But never mind; today I shall not refuse you."

He turned to his second-in-command: "See that these men have free-conduct, and give them what they asked."

The prisoners were led away, and given a tent for the night.

Vespasian kept his word. Rabbi Yochanan lived to hear the terrible news of the fall of Jerusalem; he wept and mourned the destruction of the Temple and the frightful sufferings of the Jewish people. But he lived to re-establish a Sanhedrin and Yeshivah at Yavneh, he himself acting as Nasi until Rabban Gamliel, the son of the murdered Nasi Shimon, was fit to take over.

Yavneh became the spiritual centre of the remnant of Israel. There was begun the work of arranging the oral Torah in the form that became the Mishnah. There it was ensured that Israel should not perish from the face of the earth.

The root had been saved so that the tree could grow again.

A PEARL OF GREAT PRICE

ONCE, LONG AGO, there was a Rabbi who lived some distance from a town. He had an only son, born after many years. The Rabbi's dearest wish was to see his son become great in Torah, but when he wanted to send the boy to a *melamed* the mother declared that she could not part with him even for a moment; he was all she had and it would kill her to send him away.

They nearly quarrelled, but the mother had no objection to the boy learning as much as he liked, if only he did not leave home. The father went into town to find a teacher who would agree to live with them. He met a Rabbi with whom he discussed difficult subjects, and found that the stranger was full of knowledge and had such a gift for making his meaning clear, such patience and kindness, that he was sure this would be the ideal teacher for his son both whilst he was small and later. If only he could persuade him to come out to live with them! Carefully he led the conversation round to personal things, and at last asked the stranger if he was married. Yes, he said, he had a wife. Did he have children? Yes, many. "And where are they?" The answer was strange: "They are everywhere."

It took the Rabbi only a moment to solve the riddle: "If your wife is everywhere, then you are married to the Torah and not to a woman; is not the Torah compared to a bride? If you have children everywhere, then they are your pupils, for does it not say: "He who teaches a child Torah is like a father?" Now, since you are a teacher and have no family, would you agree to come to live with us and teach my son

Torah until he is a Rabbi? I shall supply all you need whilst you are with us, and accumulate your wages so that when you are finished you will be able to live on the money all your life." The teacher agreed to stay for 25 years; during that time neither he nor the boy were to leave the homestead at all, but study Torah all day. The father promised him 1,000 gold coins, to be paid at the end of this time.

The plan succeeded from the start. The boy liked the teacher and loved to learn. Before half the years had passed, the teacher had begun to treat him as a *chaver*, and together they explored the most difficult subjects.

Eventually the time came to its end, and the father paid the teacher the promised sum. He parted from his beloved pupil with regret, but he had grown old, and now that he was wealthy he retired to a Yeshivah town to take his place amongst the elder scholars. For the young man also the time had come to settle down in some occupation or other.

First, however, he decided to have a look at the great outside world that he knew only from hearsay. Dressed in his best Rabbi's gown he set out for the town. He spent hour after hour wandering through the streets, observing the crowded bazaars, the craftsmen at their trades, the ornate public buildings.

All at once he became aware how tired he was, and hungry and thirsty too. He had had nothing since breakfast; it was now afternoon and the day was hot. Then he realised that he had brought no money. The prospect of having to trudge home for miles before he could even have a drink was appalling. He knew no one in the town whom he could ask for anything.

Then, from afar, he heard the cry of a water-seller: "Water, water! Scented with roses, cool and pleasant, refreshing for the tired, happy he who tastes it — only one penny!"

He had heard many of them that day, but this voice sounded familiar. He went in search of the man and found that he was a relative who had visited them from time to time. He asked him for a drink — but the man wanted his penny. He explained his predicament — but the man would not listen. He appealed to him and at last pointed out how much money his father had spent to make him a scholar; would he not give him a drink just out of respect for his rabbinical robe?

The more he pleaded the harder the water-seller became. "If you have studied," he said, "your wisdom is your own. If you have learned much Torah do not compliment yourself on it, for you have been created for this. God made you to learn Torah, and He made me to draw water and carry it on my back, to sell for a penny a drink and make a living for my family. No penny, no drink."

Angry and weary the young man trudged home. The more he thought of it the angrier he became. When he reached home he took off his scholar's robe and threw it on the floor. To his father he said: "All my learning cannot buy me a pennyworth of water! I want to take up a different profession."

The father got the story out of him, and then said: "Since you have decided to stop studying, I shall help you to get started in business. Upstairs in the rafters of the loft I have hidden a small casket. Inside the casket is a pearl of great value which I bought with my savings. To-morrow you shall sell it. Half the money you may have to start a business, the other half will be enough for my old age."

Next morning he told his son the exact hiding place and made him fetch the pearl. Then he gave him instructions how to sell it, and ordered him to do exactly as he had been told: "First you go to the street where they make imitation jewellery. You will see them make the shapes out of clay; when these have been baked in the furnace they plate them with lead, and finally they put on a glass lining to make them shine. In this street you will enquire for the best jewellery-makers, show them the pearl and ask them what price they would give for it — but whatever they offer, do not sell it to them.

"Next you go to the street where they sell genuine pearls. You will find there are ten shops. Show it in each shop, but do not sell it until you have heard all their offers, so you will know who makes the best offer."

The son went to town and after some hours returned, followed by porters and armed guards. He had done as his father had said. The imitation jewellery makers had offered only a few silver pieces; the gem traders had started by offering 1,000 gold pieces, but each of them had offered more than the previous one, and finally he had sold the pearl for 25,000 gold coins, and had hired the porters and guards to bring the treasure safely home. But one thing he asked his father to explain: why had he told him to go first to the imitation jewellery makers, when he knew that they would make ridiculous offers?

"I did this," replied his father, "because I wanted you to realise that if you wish to find out the value of a thing you must not go by the judgment of people who do not understand it. Only an expert can estimate a pearl.

"You were downcast because the water-seller could not appreciate the value of learning. How could he? He does not understand it. If you want to know the value of your knowledge you must go to men of wisdom. Only they can tell what your knowledge is worth."

Then he told him of a great meeting of Rabbis which was going to be held in the town that day. He was to go there and sit amongst the pupils without giving his name or showing that he recognised his father, who was going to be amongst the Rabbis.

The young man went to the meeting and listened to the proceedings. Eventually a question came up which the Rabbis discussed but could not decide. It was then that he asked to be heard. He proposed an entirely new way of solving the problem; objections were made to his argument, but he refuted them so brilliantly that in the end all the Rabbis agreed with him and issued a decision accordingly. The assembled Rabbis were so impressed by his knowledge that he was appointed a Rosh Yeshivah.

HE SLEEPS AND SLUMBERS NOT

THE MINISTERS of Tsar Nikolai the First were waiting anxiously in a spacious room in the Imperial Palace. They had been suddenly called from their homes for an Emergency Meeting. But none of them had any idea of what the emergency might be. For once all was quiet in their departments; no war, no rebellion, not even a financial crisis or international dispute that might call for urgent measures. Whatever it was, the Emperor alone knew of it.

At last the Tsar arrived. He was in one of his dangerous moods, when anyone who disagreed with him would be treated as a traitor.

He came to the point at once. "Gentlemen," he said, "I have called this meeting to settle once and for all the Jewish Question. This stubborn race is the greatest danger to the unity of Our Dominions. They refuse to speak our language, or give up any of their outlandish ways. Thus they are a State within the State. Their numbers and influence are increasing. We must get rid of this menace; I shall not be satisfied until they have either embraced our faith or left the country.

"We have planned laws to this purpose more than once. But these devils are cunning, and their bribery has often made traitors of high-placed men. There may be traitors even amongst you here."

Some of the Ministers winced. Was he going to 'expose a traitor', and 'make an example'?

"Each time," he went on, "they have gained information

about the laws before they came into force, sometimes even before they were passed, and by bribery or international protests managed to get them suppressed before they were even due to be carried out.

"It shall not happen this time. This *ukase* is going out in sealed letters to the Provincial Governors, which will not be opened until the 31st of March which is the first day of their Passover — and will then be carried out immediately. You, Gentlemen, will not leave the Palace until you have worked out the *ukase* and it has been signed. Until it comes into force you will be under secret observation, and I advise you, if you value your lives, not to meet any Jewish spies."

The Ministers were struck with fear and indignation; was this a way to speak to noblemen of Imperial Russia? But they did value their lives, and no one uttered a word of protest.

"I take it," the Tsar continued, after a glance round the table, "that we are agreed. Now for details.

"We must strike first of all at the things from which these infidels draw their strength in spite of the restrictions under which I and my predecessors have placed them, at the means by which they pass on their rebellious ideas and their fanatical religion."

He drew out a sheet of paper and read:

"*To be closed*:

(a) The Hebrew Schools known as *Heder;* proper schools may be opened provided that all teachers are Russian Christians.

(b) The Seminaries called *Yeshivoth*.

(c) The Synagogues.

(d) The Jewish baths called *Mikvah*.

To be prohibited:

(a) Circumcision.

(b) The Jewish Sabbath. All shops and factories must be opened on Saturdays, and the police must see to it that every worker or trader is doing his work on Saturdays.

To be arrested:

(a) All Rabbis.

(b) All Community Leaders.

(c) Any person who tries or might try to obstruct the carrying out of this law, or who makes protest against it."

There was silence: The Foreign Minister was thinking of what the English Newspapers would say. The Home Secretary thought of the million or two of Jews that he would have to transport to Siberia — if the thing wasn't called off first. The Minister of Justice thought of how on earth he could have such a thing in the lawbook without looking ridiculous . . .

But no one said a thing. It was no use, and highly dangerous, to answer back.

The Tsar broke into their thoughts. "It is now your task to formulate these points so as to leave no loopholes, and to give some convincing reasons for each of them. Any reference books you may need will be brought to you here, and since your work will last a number of hours I have arranged for dinner to be served in the next room. You will also find light refreshments on a table there whenever you want them.

"Now tell me," he went on in a somewhat friendlier tone, "how long do you think you will take to complete a draft?"

After a moment's silence the Prime Minister replied:

"In view of the urgency of the matter I believe my colleagues will agree to forego dinner today and be content with light refreshments during work. Even so I think we shall need 12 hours for a rough draft. As it is now 2 p.m. this means we cannot be finished until two o'clock in the morning."

"In that case," answered the Tsar, "I will not keep you any longer from your work. Tonight at two o'clock, then, I shall come and see what progress you have made. The Meeting is closed."

With these words he rose and walked out of the room.

The Ministers stood in their places for a moment. They thought many things but did no speak. It was not healthy to speak too much in the Imperial Palace.

They set to work. The Home Secretary, who had most knowledge on the subject, went over the points proposed by His Majesty. Each point was discussed, then the work was shared out between them. They found it hard work without their assistants, but by nine o'clock each had finished working out his part.

The separate sheets were read out and discussed. Some points needed changing. Each took his notes back again for a final draft. By 11.30 p.m. they had combined them into a unified document, and the Minister of Justice had begun to copy it out in clear writing.

The others sat down to a late dinner. It was only now they realised how tired and hungry they had become. Glad that the task was over, they ate heartily.

Suddenly shouted commands were heard outside. The guards were presenting arms; the Tsar was coming. They had hardly time to file into the Conference Chamber before he came in, alone.

Without a word he went to the Minister of Justice's

place, took up what he was writing and glanced through it, then through the remaining sheets. At last he gathered all the papers into a sheaf, went up to the fire place — and threw them into the flames.

Still without speaking, he walked out. The whole thing had only taken a few minutes. Outside the guards were called to attention again — he was gone.

"This is too much! " exploded the Home Secretary. "We are treated like naughty boys, first locked in to do our lines, then . . ." He pointed to the fire.

Nobody spoke in support. Indeed, the Home Secretary seemed to regret that he had spoken.

"It seems," began the Finance Minister, "that His Majesty does not require our services any more tonight. I move, therefore, that we adjourn."

The Prime Minister turned on him. "I cannot agree at all," he said. "His Majesty has not dismissed us. It is certainly clear that he is displeased with our draft. If so it is our duty to prepare a better one, certainly not to leave our posts."

"But on what lines," retorted the Finance Minister, "do you propose to plan a new draft? This one was based on His Majesty's own wishes. If that was not good, how can other ideas satisfy His Majesty better?"

To this the Prime Minister had nothing to say.

At last it was agreed that they would stay until 2 a.m., the time originally stated, in case the Tsar would return with new proposals. In the meantime they would go on with their interrupted dinner.

Food and wine restored their good humour, and they were drinking one toast after another, when shortly before 2 o'clock they heard again the commands outside and the Tsar returned, with two Adjutants.

He too was in a genial mood. "Well, Gentlemen," he addressed them, "so you have finished the work and started celebrating? I thought it couldn't take all that long. Now, if you are ready, I'd like to see the draft."

Astonishment and confusion were in the expressions of the Ministers. At last the Prime Minister brought out: "B-but . . . Your Majesty did inspect the d-draft at midnight, and . . ."

He broke off when he saw the Tsar's sudden gesture of anger and disgust. "Is there," demanded the Tsar in an icy tone, "Is there one amongst you Gentlemen sober enough to tell me what this man is babbling about?"

The Ministers looked to the War Minister, who was regarded as a favourite of the Tsar, and he addressed his master in his most conciliatory manner:

"Your Imperial Majesty! If we have incurred Your Majesty's displeasure by having dinner whilst waiting for new orders, we most humbly apologise, but when your Majesty rejected the original draft we thought . . ."

"What on earth," interrupted the Tsar, "are you talking about?"

The War Minister tried to rally his dignity. "Does not Your Majesty please to remember that shortly before midnight Your Majesty inspected the draft we had completed, and burned it? We were awaiting further orders, and in the meantime . . ."

The Tsar's anger was mounting. "Are you suggesting that I have been here before? Is that what all of you say?"

The Ministers affirmed this.

"A conspiracy!" thundered the Tsar. "By Heaven, a conspiracy! The whole Cabinet bought by the Jews! But they must be mad to sit here feasting all this time and then tell me the most stupid lie ever invented. Von Gradewitz," he addressed one of Adjutants, "call the guards and have these men locked up until I decide whether they belong in the mad-house or in Siberia."

Obediently the Adjutant went to the door. A platoon of guards marched in and stood awaiting orders.

The Tsar had changed back to his cold, ironic mood. He said in French: "Messieurs les Ministres, I know that in your hearts you think of me as a tyrant; but let none of you say that you have been condemned without fair trial and evidence. Von Gradewitz, ask these plain honest soldiers whether these gentlemen are lying or I myself!"

Gradewitz spoke to the sergeant of the guard. "Has anyone entered this building since you came on duty?"

"No one, Sir," replied the soldier, "except His Majesty alone."

"Fool!" countered Gradewitz, "we know that His Majesty entered, or he would not be here! I asked you if anyone came in before this."

"Yes, Sir," answered the man, "and that was what I said His Majesty came here, alone, at ten minutes to twelve, stayed for three minutes, and left again."

"An impostor!" exclaimed the Tsar, who had turned white with anger and fear. "A traitor can impersonate me, and walk past my guards unchallenged! Damnation, what have we come to! Call the Officer of the Day!"

He whispered to Gradewitz, then stepped behind a heavy curtain. When the officer came in Gradewitz asked him: "Have you seen His Majesty the Tsar tonight?"

"Yes," replied the Officer, "I saw His Majesty twice. The first time just before twelve, and again just now."

"Are you quite sure?" asked Gradewitz. "I happen to know that His Majesty did not leave his apartments from ten o'clock until now. Could it have been someone impersonating His Majesty?"

"Impossible," declared the Officer, "quite impossible. I opened the doors for His Majesty myself on both occasions, and you will agree that it is my business to know His Majesty's appearance. Besides, I had to ask him for the password."

"And he gave it?" asked Gradewitz.

"Naturally," said the Officer, "why should His Majesty not know his own password?"

"Enough! " said the Tsar, stepping out from behind the curtain. He bared his head reverently.

"Gentlemen," he said in solemn tones, "at twelve o'clock I was asleep in my room. But the Guardian of Israel does not sleep or slumber. The man you saw was His Heavenly messenger sent to hold us back from an ill-considered step. I bow to His will. Gentlemen, the *Ukase* is withdrawn! "

THE TENTH JEW

IN THE SECOND generation of Chassidism (latter half of 18th century) there lived in the town of Rovno (Ukraine) a Rabbi known as Reb Leib Sore's, one of the "hidden" Tzaddikim. Much of his time was spent travelling and collecting money for *pidyon shvuyim* (to free people unjustly imprisoned), and other important, often secret, purposes.

Once, a few days before Yom Kippur, he was staying for the night in a village, when heavy rains set in, rapidly converting the primitive roads into mere stretches of mud. The traveller was enquiring if anyone would still try to drive to the town where he had meant to spend Yom Kippur, when he was told that there would be a minyan in the village. Eight Jewish men and boys lived in the place, and two men were to come in from a hamlet in the midst of the forest. There was a Sefer Torah too. He took it that it was God's will that he should pray with these country Jews.

On Erev Yom Kippur, having gone for *tvilah* in the river, he went to the improvised shool and prepared his soul for the *minchah* prayer. The eight local Jews gathered, but they had to *daven minchah* without *minyan,* as the two guests had not yet arrived. They dispersed again to take the *s'udah mafseketh.*

His meal finished, the Rabbi went back to shool, put on his *kittel* and *talith,* and immersed himself in the private prayers before Kol Nidre. Suddenly he realised a change in the room. The men were talking worriedly; the sun had gone down, it was becoming time for Kol Nidre, but the two had not arrived.

Then the door opened; but the man in muddy sheepskin coat and cap, who had come, was no Jew.

"*Panka* Rifka sends me," he began, in the Ukrainian dialect known as "Goyish".

"Yossel and Moshka were taken away this morning. The gendarme arrested them, for stealing, but Rifka says it isn't true. She is crying all the time, and says you should pray for them."

Weeping started in the next room, where the women had assembled. Then the room was filled with babble, several people trying simultaneously to drag more information out of the peasant, whilst others were discussing possible developments. Only the Rabbi did not take part. He was standing in his corner, whispering: "Master of the world, I thank You for making me stay here. Since this is Your purpose, I rely on You to help me set them free soon. But must I really pray without a minyan on this holy day?"

A moment later, he raised his voice: "Yiden, let us not forget the message sent to us. We were asked to pray for them, not talk or think of ways to help them. That can be done later. First we must pray, for I tell you that their being arrested just today, of all the days in the year, means that their case is now, today, being considered in the High Court above. Our prayers, as well as their own, will decide the issue. Let us then begin Kol Nidre with a humble, broken heart."

The men obeyed at once, and Kol Nidre was said with more than usual feeling.

After Kol Nidre the Rabbi again addressed them: "I have a feeling that we may still have a minyan for *maariv*. Where have the men been taken to?"

A man answered: "The goy says they were taken to Rovno."

"If so," replied the Rabbi, "it is not they who will make up our minyan. Has anyone been expecting another guest?"

No-one had. — "Does anyone know of another Jew living round here? Someone, perhaps who doesn't mix with Jews? Is there a *meshumad* in this village?" — "A meshumad!" exclaimed several men at once. — "Certainly," said the Rabbi, "why not a meshumad? Can't he do *teshuvah*? Haven't we just said 'We give permission to pray with the sinners'? — Is there a meshumad, then?"

The oldest man spoke up. "Yes, Rabbi, there is one here. It is fifty years, that a poor young man settled here. He wore modern dress, and he took liberties with many laws. He was clever though. He had learnt a little; also he could write Polish and Russian. The poritz (squire) engaged him as a clerk. Then the poritz's only daughter fell in love with him, and he — be his name wiped out — sold his faith for the poritz's gold. For that boy is now the poritz, and a worse hater of Israel than any *schlachtzitz*."

"And what became of the woman?" asked the Rabbi.

"She died long ago. No one is left but that meshumad, and he lives all alone with his servant. He is hard with his tenants, and doesn't even visit his neighbour *pritzim*."

The Rabbi closed his eyes for a moment. Then he said, quietly, but with a curious tone of emphasis: "He sold himself, did you say? . . . And it is Yom Kippur of the fiftieth year? . . . Isn't that a fitting time for a slave to be set free? 'And you shall return, each man to his heritage, and each to the family of his fathers . . .' We must try it. Where is his mansion?"

"You want to go to him?" wondered the other. "He will have you thrown to the dogs!" — "Don't worry about me," replied the Rabbi. "A *shliach mitzvah* has special protection.

But pray that I may succeed. Pray for that poor lost soul, and forgive him your personal complaints. If I should not be back in half an hour, start *maariv* without me."

With that he strode to the door, still in his kittel and talith. He asked a boy to point out the way, then disappeared into the night.

Silence was in the room. After a while they opened their *machzorim,* and found some prayers to say. They were still sitting thus, trying to drown their perplexity in the *tfilla zakkah,* when suddenly the Rabbi's voice began, in the sad, sweet, Yom Kippur tune: *"Borchu* . . ." They had responded before it occured to them to wonder how and when he had come back, or how there had come to be a minyan. But there was the tenth man, in the south-east corner; a tall, gaunt figure hidden in a talith. And from under the talith showed the knees of blue velvet breeches, white silk hose, and black patent leather shoes that went with the costume of the gentry of the period.

And the simple men trembled . . .

Trembling still, they followed their self-chosen *chazan* through the Service. Never, even on Yom Kippur, had they prayed like this before. Their tears flowed freely, their hearts were humble; when they came to confess their sins, they found so many they had never thought of as sins, yet they found themselves willing to repent and mend their ways. Was not a greater miracle of *teshuvah* going on in this very room? And somehow they felt that the achievement of forgiveness for themselves was bound up with that of the poritz, and they reached out to help him.

When the Rabbi intoned: "May He raise up our prayers of evening . . .," they felt themselves lifted up strangely. When he said: "For like clay in the hand of the potter are we in Thy hand . . .," they saw how crooked their souls had become in the bitter struggle for survival, and besought The Potter to make them over . . .

When they left, late at night, the strangers were still standing in their corners. In the morning, they found the two in earnest conversation, and kept away from them, until the Rabbi began the prayers. All day the poritz remained on his feet, his face to the wall, swaying in prayer, now and then shaking with sobs.

When night came on, and they said the *Sheymoth,* the poritz put his head into the open *aron hakodesh,* and cried, ever more loudly: God is the true God!

And with the seventh time, he collapsed.

The Rabbi stayed for the *Baal Teshuvah's* burial. Then he set out to work for the release of the arrested men.

THE PRICE OF AN ETHROG

Reb Itzig was walking with his head bent against the rain, which the wind was driving across the exposed field path. His heart was as heavy as his feet. Business had been bad again today. The heavy autumn rains had made many roads in these Hungarian flatlands impassable. Some villages were completely cut off. In others the peasants were too busy protecting their barns and saving what they could from exposed stacks to think of trading with him.

And there were only a few days to Succoth! There would be no new clothes for his family this time.

He was amongst the bare fields of his village now. Soon he would warm himself in front of the fire. Thank heaven he had been able in time to barter some merchandise for a load of wood. He needed some warmth now. He wondered about the approaching frosts; would he be able to walk out in his bald sheepskin coat another winter?

One thing at least was safe. He had his Ethrog and Lulav already. And what an Ethrog! Ripe, yellow and spotless! But it looked as if he would be the only one in the village. The rain that had impaired his living here had cut the railways lower down, and the Ethrogim had not yet arrived. He was glad now that he had accepted the Ethrog offered him four weeks ago, which the dealer had received as a sample. Itzig had been doubtful at first, afraid it might spoil before the Festival; and the dealer owed him a good Ethrog, one of the finest he could get. That had been the agreement they had made two years ago, when Ethrogim had been so dear that Itzig could only afford one by sharing with neighbours. It was then he had determined that never again would he miss an Ethrog for lack of money. Ever since then he had paid the dealer six kreutzer every Friday on the understanding that he would get an Ethrog Mehudar every year regardless of the current price and pay any balance later.

And now the whole Community might have to be *yotze* with his Ethrog, the Ethrog of the poor hawker who sat behind the Almemor!

To be sure, the dealer had tried to buy it back, had offered fantastic prices. He had gone up to 40 gulden. 40 gulden! What Itzig could have bought with 40 gulden! But he had refused. He would not sell such a *Mitzvah* for a 100 gulden!

And Zirel, his wife, had agreed. She needed a new dress urgently, and things for the children, but she understood the value of a Mitzvah too.

A good wife. She did not complain if things were hard. She understood. She would not ask about the day's business. She would guess it, and say nothing. But she would have a glass of tea for him in no time, she would make him comfortable, tell him something clever his little Rivkale had said, or what the Melamed thought of Shimela's reading. All the same, it was hard to come home empty-handed.

Here was his cottage; he had hoped to be able to rebuild the north wall this year. It would have to wait...

His wife greeted him cheerfully enough, but from the start Itzig sensed something in the air. When he had started sipping his tea, he asked his wife what was the matter.

"Oh, Itzig," replied Zirel. "I have worried so much. The Ethrog dealer has been again, and this time he has brought three Baale Battim — from Debrecen. They have no Ethrogim there at all, so the Rosh Hakohol has sent Gaboim to all the Kehilloth in the district to buy one at any price."

"Well," said Itzig, "you know that we are not selling ours; you told them so, didn't you?" He sat up tensely.

"Of course I told them, but they pressed me so hard... They offered a 100 gulden from the start, and then they offered more, laying it all out on the table, all those banknotes and goldpieces... It made my head swim to see it."

"I hope you did not give in?" interupted Itzig anxiously. "We could not sell a Mitzvah for money! And besides, the whole Kehillah would be without an Ethrog!"

"No, thank God, I did not sell it, though it was very hard to refuse. They put 400 gulden on the table in the end. And the arguments! 400 gulden! God forgive me, I am only a weak woman; but I told them I would do nothing without you, and they had to be content with that. They wanted to leave the money on the table, but I scolded them and they took it back. I would have gone mad with all this money in the house." She began to cry. Itzig reassured her. "Now, now, Zirel, calm yourself. You did a great mitzvah; not many would have had the strength."

"It was very wrong of them to press you," he continued when she was calmer. "You could not have given in to them if you had wanted to. They could not be *yotze* with the Ethrog if you had sold it against my wishes. We cannot sell our Mitzvah. There would be no *broche* in such money. It is only a temptation sent to try us."

There was a knock at the door. A man's voice called: "May I come in? Reb Itzig is in now, isn't he?"

"Yes, come in!" answered Itzig. The man entered. He was tall and stout, his greying beard fell over a new-looking silk gabardine.

"Ah, Reb Mendel! Sholem Alechem!" Itzig greeted him. "Take a seat. You came with the other gaboim?"

"Alechem Sholem" answered the newcomer, "Yes, we came about the Ethrog. But your wife could not decide without you. Have you thought it over?"

"I do not have to think," answered Itzig, with some sharpness. "I am sorry if you have no Ethrog, but you cannot have ours. You can save your words; there is nothing more to be said about it."

"Well, well," Reb Mendel calmed him. "I thought as much myself, but the others would not believe me. Do you know any place where we can find an Ethrog?"

Itzig did not, and after they had talked a while of some local events, Reb Mendel got up to go. Itzig accompanied him.

"One more thing," said Reb Mendel when they were outside. "I am glad I came here, even if I did not get an Ethrog. I have never met anyone with such devotion to a mitzvah as you and your wife. And listen to an old man; after this, God will send you prosperity. He could keep us all comfortable if we were worthy, but not everyone can resist the temptations that riches bring. You have shown that money cannot corrupt you, and I am sure you will have plenty of it soon. Now let me give you ten gulden. — No, don't refuse. I don't meant it as a gift. Return it when you don't need it any longer. The wheel turns, you know; and if ever I, or my children, fall on bad times, you will help them in return."

With this he went away, and Itzig stood holding the banknote.

Well, that was enough to make a comfortable Yom Tov anyway. And as Reb Mendel had said, he did not have to regard it as a gift.

He went in and told his wife. But she was not as delighted

as he had thought she would be, and went about her work silently. At last he asked her what worried her now.

She sat down by him. "Look, Itzig," she explained, "I know that I had to do what I did. I had to leave the decision to you. But all along I have been wondering if you were doing right. You should at least have asked a *Shaalah*. We ask Shaaloth on smaller things than this. If you had told the Rav what 400 gulden mean to us, how much good can be done for us and others with all that money, maybe he would have decided otherwise. That is what worries me."

Itzig considered it. "There is something in what you say; but it does not need a Shaalah. The position is so clear! On one hand I have a Mitzvah, a Mitzvah that one can fulfil only once a year. On the other hand I have 400 gulden. Here is cold, dead money, and there is the living word of God. Is there any doubt what one must choose?"

He thought for a moment.

"And yet," he went on, "if you like, I shall ask a Shaalah even now. But not of the Rav. I shall ask a Shaalah of God!"

She looked up at him, astonished: "What do you mean?"

"Look, Reb Mendel has given us ten gulden; and he said he feels sure we shall be rich soon. You say maybe we should have taken the 400 gulden. Now, even five gulden are enough to carry us over Yom Tov. We could buy a lottery ticket with the rest, and if God really wants us to be rich, He can give us the money in this way. And if we do not win, we shall have lost our five gulden, but at least we shall know that we are not meant to be rich, so that we did right in refusing to sell the Ethrog."

His wife was satisfied with this solution, and next morning Itzig bought a five gulden ticket for the State Lottery. The other five were spent on Yom Tov preparations.

Succoth came, and a strange Succoth it was. Itzig and

his family got up early to *bensh* Ethrog in their Succah, for the Shammes was waiting already to take their Ethrog round the houses so that the women could also fulfil the Mitzvah.

In shul prayers took even longer than usual, for everybody had to make *brocho* on Itzig's Ethrog. In Hallel too, many made the *Na'anuim* with this one Ethrog. Thus Itzig's seat below the Almemor became for the moment the centre of the Congregation. But though Itzig was glad of the *zechuth* that had come through him, he showed no conceit, so no one felt humiliated or envious.

But he was uneasy in his mind. He did not allow himself to regret his refusal of the money, but he wondered if he had been right to buy the lottery ticket. It was not likely that he would win anything, so probably he had wasted a lot of good money. But supposing he did win — and after all, he was hoping for that — would that not mean that he would receive the reward for the mitzvah in this world, and get nothing for it in the world to come? Again, this clever idea of "asking a Shaalah of God" did not look so clever to him now. It looked to him very much like "testing God", the sin for which the Jewish people had been so heavily punished in the wilderness.

At last he took his problem to the Rav. The learned man listened to him, and after considering for a moment said: "Reb Itzig, you have nothing to worry about. I wish people would do 'sins' like this every day. 'Testing God' means a case when someone doubts the power, or the love of God and demands a miracle to prove it. But according to what you told me you did not doubt God, but only your own worthiness.

"Also, a lottery win is not exactly a miracle, for someone who would not want to believe would still call it 'chance'. Although in truth, you know, it's exactly the opposite. I have heard this from my Rabbi, on whom be Peace: 'The less you can influence the outcome of a thing, and the less it seems to depend on the so-called laws of Nature, the clearer is the hand of God in it.'

"The people who talk of Chance as if it could decide anything are only cheating themselves, for 'chance' means something happening without a natural cause to decide it, so how can they call it a cause in itself?"

That last part was too deep for Itzig, but the main thing was that there was no sin in what he had done. But what about the reward of his mitzvah, he still wanted to know.

"Well," replied the Rav, "I can tell you on what this question depends.

"If a person wants the things of this world, money, honours or enjoyments, for their own sake, and he does even his mitzvoth in order to get such things, then his reward is paid off in this world. But if he serves God with a pure heart, and he wants money and other things only in order to be able to do more mitzvoth, then God gives them to him not as payment for his good deeds, but in order to help him to do more of them.

"Which of these applies to you, no man can tell you for sure, for only God sees the heart. But one can tell a lot from the outcome: if you win something, and you find that afterwards you are doing more mitzvoth, and learn more Torah than before, then you can assume that it was sent as a help, and not as paying-off of mitzvoth.

"Anyway," he continued with a smile, "this shaalah is not a practical one yet. You haven't won yet. I hope from my heart, though, that you do win something. I should be glad to know that you have parnossoh more comfortably."

With this blessing the Rabbi sent Itzig home; but for a long time he sat wondering about the odd things people may do. Fancy this Itzig, who barely made a living, putting five gulden into the Lottery! In the end, however, he told himself that simple men, in their innocence, may succeed where wiser ones would not dare to begin. Itzig deserved to win a prize for his trust in God alone. "I should certainly like to know the end of this! " he muttered. Then he turned to his Gemoro again.

To Itzig, his Shaalah was serious and practical enough. That evening, after Shemone Esreh, he said a private prayer: "Please, God, nobody knows if it is good for me to win, but You know. I pray You, if it is not good for me or my children, don't let me win."

He felt better after that. And to make a start, he resolved firmly that of whatever he might win, much or little, he would give right away not a tenth but a fifth part for Charity.

With a lighter heart he enjoyed Shmini Atzereth, and on Simchath Torah he felt joyous as never before.

On the day after, he went out again with his sack, the peacefulness of the holidays still in him. He made a few sales, and was thankful. He felt that God was helping him.

He was wondering, however, what had become of his Lottery ticket. Days passed and the drawing must have taken place already. Since he hadn't heard of it, he probably had lost.

One evening, as he was getting nearer home, he saw a small boy standing near the first house, then running towards him. It was his Shima'le. Breathlessly the boy told him that the lottery agent had been to the house, and that they had won a lot of money. "Mammy is quite ill from it! " he added. "She sent me to look out for you."

In the street people stopped to congratulate him, but he hurried home. He found his wife still very excited, and dabbing at her eyes. With difficulty she managed to tell him that they had indeed won, and the first prize! A hundred thousand gulden! He calmed her, and said: "Don't worry, Zirel, God gave us strength to live in poverty, now He will give us strength to be rich." Then he spoke the blessing "Ha-tov ve-ha-maitiv."

The next day he travelled to the district town to receive the money. When he was putting it into a bank, on the advice of Reb Mendel, he insisted on keeping twenty thousand in a separate account. That was his Charity account, and he soon distributed almost half of it to people and organisations in the district. The other half he kept in the account, for the time being, to be distributed later.

He decided to move to Vienna. He felt it was not good for him and his family that he should be the richest man for many miles around.

In Vienna he found good friends who advised him how to invest his money. He had sound business sense himself, and became a successful financier. But never did he spend less than five hours a day in learning Torah, and never was a deserving cause or person sent away empty-handed from his house.

One peculiarity remained with him all his long life: Every Succoth he had to have the very best Ethrog that money could buy. He would spend hours and hours selecting them, and often he would buy a dozen from different sources before he was satisfied. When his friends chaffed him about this, he would reply: "Ah, but you don't know the value of an Ethrog. I do."

GHOSTLY CLOCK

THIS HAPPENED before the war. I was the Rabbi of an East End congregation then.

One morning an elderly couple came to see me. One could see right away that something was the matter, and not something that had happened, but something about to happen; they were in a state of terror. It is nothing unusual for a Rav to meet people in trouble; it is part of his job. And trouble was not unusual in the East End. I expected to hear about a notice to quit, or the bailiffs coming, possibly even about a son in trouble with the Police. But what I heard was something unexpected.

"You must help us, Rabbi!" said the man. "We can't bear it any longer. We shall not go back into our house until you do something."

"But what is the matter?" I asked.

"We can't stay in our house." said the woman. "There is a *shed* (demon) in the house! Oh, I can't think what has brought this on us! Please come and do something! Perhaps you can drive it away by prayer. Or if you can't, you must find us somewhere to go to. We must find some other place to stay."

It took me some time to make them realise that I did not understand what had happened. At last they calmed down sufficiently to talk in connected sentences and answer questions. Or rather the man answered, his wife sitting there in mute despair, and only now and then taking part in the conversation.

"Now tell me what happened." I began.

"I have told you" he said. "There is a *shed* in the house. The place isn't safe. It throws things around."

"When does it do it?" I asked. "All the time?"

"No," answered the man, "only at night. When we go to bed everything is quiet, but in the middle of the night there is a crash in the kitchen, and when I get up to see, there is no-one in the room and the clock is on the floor. It's the same night after night. First I thought we hadn't put it on the mantelpiece properly, so the next night I put it there myself, two inches from the edge; and last night I put it right to the wall. But it only made the crash come a bit later. At four o'clock this morning there was the same crash again, and the clock again on the floor, in the same spot. I don't know what he should have against our clock. He must do it just to wake us and give us a scare."

"Who is 'he'?" I asked.

"The *shed,* of course," said the man.

"Could it be some neighbour playing a practical joke on you?" I suggested.

"Impossible!" he asserted. "The people in the house are all nice, respectable people. We have known them for years, and they wouldn't do such a thing. Besides, they couldn't get in if they wanted to. There is a patent lock on the door."

"Does anyone live with you in the flat?" I enquired.

"No," was the answer, "we are quite alone. Our children are married and have homes of their own. We don't want to live together with them if we can help it. I know these young people. Old parents visiting once a week, and maybe bringing something for the children, that's alright; but to be with them all the time — it would be no life."

I was stumped. Many "ghost stories" may be just lies, made up to make some old place interesting, or to frighten somebody. But these people were obviously telling the truth. Still, I could not believe in this demon of theirs. Not because it would be against what is called natural laws. There are many "supernatural" things. But it just didn't make sense. If only there had been some meaning in it, if it had been an article connected with some great wrong, for instance, I might possibly conceive that something spiritual which most people only know in the form of conscience could sometimes cause a concrete happening, to remind those responsible of an unforgiven guilt. But what meaning could there be in an ordinary clock falling down in an ordinary home?

Again, some "ghosts" may be the products of an oversensitive imagination. When you lie sleepless, the ticking of your watch, the minute tinkle of a spring in your bed reacting to an imperceptible movement, even the throbbing of your own temple artery against the cushion — things like these, unnoticeable in the daytime, can assume gigantic proportions. And then there are noises of unknown origin. At one time I used to be startled by distant, semihuman shrieks, until their regularity convinced me that they came from a sawmill. I could conceive people imagining ghosts behind such strange, though natural, noises.

But these people spoke of hard, objective facts, seen in bright electric light. Was there after all something supernatural here?

Like a detective despairing of a case but still groping for clues, I went on asking for details: "Have you a cat?"

"No." he answered.

"Could a cat get in from outside?"

"No, the window was closed."

I tried in a different direction: "What sort of clock is it?"

"An alarm clock." explained the man. "Not one of those new-fangled ones. An old alarm clock, big and heavy, with a strong loud bell on top. And a good clock it is. I have had it for years and years and it never gave trouble."

Here his wife interrupted: "The way he goes on about that shabby old clock of his! If I had my way I'd have bought a new one long ago. Now it has even lost one of its feet, and I must pick it up each time I want to see the time. It's a disgrace to the room. Maybe its falling down is a sign that it isn't right to keep the thing in the house."

"You leave my clock alone!" exclaimed her husband. "It has served me so long, it would be sinful to throw it away now. What if it has grown old! So have I, and I don't want to be thrown on the scrapheap either. And if it has lost a foot — you have lost your teeth, haven't you?"

Some tactful interruption was overdue; I went on with my questions: "So you keep it on the mantelpiece?"

"Yes," replied the man. "I used to take it to the bedroom at night, of course, to wake me for work, but now that I'm retired we leave it on the mantelpiece in the kitchen."

The wife had another objection to make: "But it isn't always on the mantelpiece. By day I keep it on the cupboard; my eyes are not as strong as they used to be, so I must have it near. And now, of course, that it can't stand up, I must have it handy to pick up."

"So you keep it on the mantelpiece, and it can't stand up..." I repeated, rather at a loss what to think.

Then suddenly I saw daylight.

"And on which side does it lie?" I asked. "On its face or on its back?"

They could not answer this at once. By day, of course, it lay on its back, so they could see the time. But at night?

I brought my own clock, put it on the desk on its back, and let them put it on the mantelpiece in turn. They laid it on its back.

"Well," I declared, "before I can decide whether or not it is a *shed* you must make one more trial: go home, and tonight lay the clock on its face."

"But" argued the woman, "are we to stay in that house overnight? I'm sure I won't sleep a wink!"

"You can be assured" I told her, "that nothing will happen to you. Nothing has ever happened except to the clock, and I am nearly certain that to-morrow it will be where you left it."

"Oh, if you could promise that!" she exclaimed.

"I can't promise it," I said, "but — although I am against betting as a rule I am prepared to bet you twenty shillings to one that nothing will happen."

"So sure are you?" she said with evident relief. "In that case we'll give it another chance."

They went home, and next morning came back with happy faces.

"It worked, Rabbi!" the man shouted.

"How did you do it, without even going there?"

"Well," I explained, "I was not absolutely certain. But, you see, your clock was lying on its back, and maybe the winding-keys stick out, and one of them, of course, is slowly turning all the time... You see? It just rolled along on the tip of the key till it reached the edge..."

BURIED TREASURE

SO FAR the holiday had been a wash-out. Even when it did not rain the waves whipped in by the strong west wind made swimming dangerous. Reuven, a Yeshiva student of two years standing, had been kicking himself for coming to Cornwall with his parents and Shimon his school-boy brother instead of going to Camp with his friends.

There was just one thing that might save the holiday. They had been waiting for a low tide to reach and explore the cave isolated behind the headland which local people called the "smugglers' cave" or "treasure cave". It was supposed to be dangerous in stormy weather, and they had not told their parents of their plan, as they might have been anxious.

At last low tide had come round in mid-morning. The brothers had ostensibly gone out for a walk but doubled back and made their way to the cave, loaded with all the equipment they had secretly gathered and hidden.

Using their torches they had explored every space amongst the wet boulders but had not found anything exciting. There remained the ledge high up one side behind which they had seen a hollow space. Reuven tied their rope to an iron bar and after many throws succeeded in anchoring it.

With much heaving and scrambling they reached the top, but exploration showed nothing of interest. There was indeed a sheltered hollow, dark and damp, in which you could imagine a smuggler hiding his treasures. They would have to be small treasures however — there was no room for cases of brandy or bales of tobacco.

Moreover they were not the first explorers by a long way. The wall was covered with stupid inscriptions: "Roy was here," "L.V. and M.B." (surrounded by a heart), and so on. Well, at least they could leave their own mark behind. They decided to make it a Hebrew one: ראובן ושמעון אחים, תש״ך.

With his pocket knife Reuven started to carve on a smooth part of the wall at the back of the hollow, whilst Shimon held the torch.

Suddenly, as Shimon moved the torch, Reuven noticed just where he was writing, some peculiar letters — certainly not English ones. Fantastic as it seemed, he could have sworn that he had seen a ב ,ח and a ש.

Excitedly they looked for more. There was a long inscription. The letters were very faint, but just recognisable if you held the torch at a particular angle. They were of a peculiar spidery shape, but definitely Hebrew square writing.

With Shimon shining the torch by his directions, Reuven traced the inscription and copied it onto a piece of paper.

After long work he had this:

אנ. יוסי מ..ר לודים תל.יד .בי יוחנן נמכר.. משבי יר.. לים עבד
לחפור בדיל בבר..ניה בחסדי המקום בר.תי ונחב.ת. בין הבריטני.
כמה שנ.. ועכש. שמ.תי ש..ומיים שמעו עלי את כל מ.. יש לי
גנזתי ..חורי הסלע המוצ. .מסרנו לבי. .נסת ויגיד לרבי שלא
שכ. תי יראת ש׳ ולא את תורתו ויתפל. . לי

In spite of the missing letters he eventually made out the meaning:

> "I, Yosi from the village of Luddim, pupil of Rabbi Yochanan, was sold from the captivity of Jerusalem as a slave to dig tin in Britain, By G-d's grace, I escaped and hid amongst the Britons for several years. And now I have heard that the Romans have heard about me. All my possessions I have hidden behind the boulder. He who finds it

> should hand it over to a Synagogue, and tell my Rabbi that I have not forgotten the fear of the Almighty, nor His Torah, and pray for me."

Overwhelmed, the boys considered what they had found. "Imagine!" exclaimed Shimon, "a Jew here, back in the time of Churban Beth Hamikdosh! And he had learned Torah -- I wonder who his 'Rabbi Yochanan' was."

"I should think it was Rabbi Yochanan Ben Zakkai," answered Reuven. "You must have heard how he saved the Yeshiva of Yavneh and became *Nossi* until Rabbi Gamliel was old enough to succeed his father, who had been killed in the Churban."

"And who was this Yosi?" asked Shimon.

"I have never heard about him. But then he was captured as a talmid, so he didn't become a teacher, and you wouldn't expect any sayings of his to be reported."

"And what became of him, do you think?"

"Who knows?" replied Reuven. "Maybe he escaped, maybe the Romans got him in the end . . . He may even have died hiding in this cave . . ."

"Ooh!" exclaimed Shimon. "Don't say that! I wouldn't like to share a cave with a skeleton . . ."

"Now don't be silly!" expostulated Reuven. "There is hardly a chance of our finding any bones even if he did die here. And if we did, we would have a great Mitzvah getting him buried. But perhaps he escaped . . .

"Anyway, let's start looking for his treasure. Now which boulder did he mean? Probably it was that big one . . ."

Just then the torch went dim. The battery was used up and no amount of coaxing would get more than a dim glow out of it.

"We must get home", said Reuven, "and come back with a new battery, and spades."

But when they looked down in the dim daylight filtering in, they saw that the floor was flooded. They must have spent hours up here, and the tide had come in. There was no hope of swimming home along the rock-strewn shore — they could hear the wind howling outside.

"Wha . . . What's going to happen?" shivered Shimon, on the verge of tears.

What indeed, thought Reuven. Their parents did not know where they were. Low tide would be about midnight. They might try finding their way back in the night . . . There would be no moon, for it was near Rosh Chodesh . . . If they starved here, the secret would die with them . . .

"Let us pray for help! " he said.

Together they said all the chapters of Tehillim that Reuven knew by heart. Then they prayed, asking to be saved, and ended by saying: "In the *Zechuth* of Yosi and of his teacher Rabbi Yochanan Ben Zakkai! "

For some time nothing happened, only the wind howling, the light growing less, and bigger waves coming into the cave.

Then from afar came shouts: "Roo-ven! Shee-mon! Where are you?" It must be their father searching for them — outside in a boat. They shouted, but their voices only went echoing round the cave. From outside their names were called again and again, but further away now.

At last they decided to slide down the rope and wading in the icy water up to their armpits reached the cave mouth. There, a hundred yards away, were two men in a rowing boat. This time their shouts were heard and the boys were rescued.

Next day, with their father, they dug behind the great boulder. They brought to light a large number of slates, which turned out to be inscribed with a kind of Mishnayoth, starting: "Since I have no one whom to repeat it to, I shall write down all I have heard from Rabbi Yochanan Ben Zakkai . . ."

It made a great stir in the papers and experts came from everywhere. The Government claimed the finds as treasure trove, but Reuven appeared in Court and claimed that according to the inscription he, the finder, had the duty of handing them over to a Synagogue. So in the end they became the property of his Yeshiva, but since the contents were published, they really became the possession of all who learn.

S . . . O . . . S . .

REUVEN was walking fast. He hoped he would not be late for dinner. This was the first Rosh Hashana his father had allowed him to pray in the Yeshivah; it was a long way to walk and he didn't want the family to wait for him.

But it had been worth going all this way. He was sure he had prayed better than ever before in the company of the Rabbis and their students. And the Shofar blowing! Reuven had learned the laws of Shofar and practised a little, and he knew how hard it was to get the tones right. His own teacher, Rabbi Silberman, had blown the Shofar perfectly today . . .

What was this? Somebody was blowing Shofar somewhere in the street through which he was walking. There was no Shul round here. It must be someone blowing for a person too ill to go to Shul. Certainly it wasn't a child practising — the tones came correctly without any false starts.

And yet there was something wrong with the notes. As it grew louder Reuven followed the notes. Shevorim, Tekioh, Tekioh, Tekioh, again, — this was on too many — Shevorim, then a pause. Why was there no Tekioh after this Shevorim? It started again: Shevorim, 3 Tekios, Shevorim — then it stopped.

"What is going on?" Reuven thought. This was not proper blowing at all. But it reminded him of something . . . He stopped and listened. Here it came again. Three short, three long, three short . . . Why, that was S.O.S.! Somebody must be in danger! He ran towards the sound. What could it be? Someone attacked by a burglar? But in broad daylight! The street was perfectly quiet. The few passers-by had paid no attention to the sounds, but looked curiously at him when he started to run. Could it be someone imprisoned, kidnapped? "Don't be silly!" he told himself. These things don't happen in an ordinary street."

He stopped at the house from which he thought the sounds had come. It had a Mezuzah. He knocked firmly. The blowing started again — he was sure now it came from this house, but no one answered the door, Three short, three long, short . . . it had stopped! Something must have happened to whoever was sending the signal. He must get in at once! He climbed on to the windowsill, but the window would not open. In a panic, Reuven kicked at the glass. It broke, and he felt a stabbing pain in his leg, but without stopping he kicked out more fragments and climbed in. Inside all was quiet. An ordinary dining room, a shelf of Seforim, the table laid for a festive dinner.

Doubt assailed him. Perhaps he was wrong, perhaps no one had called for help at all and he had made a fool of himself. An expensive foolishness too — he would have to pay for the glass, and do a lot of explaining for breaking in. Who would believe his story?

And he had definitely cut his leg on the glass — a bloodstain was forming on the carpet. Should he make a bolt for it?

No, having gone this far, he must find out what was wrong. In his own mind he was still certain that what he had heard was a call for help, and had come from this house.

He opened the door to the hall — there was a smell of gas! So something was wrong after all!

Holding his breath, he dashed to the kitchen. There was a back door which he threw open. A kettle of water was standing on the cooker, a gas tap was half on, but no flame. He turned off the gas, then ran out of the back door and drew a deep breath.

But who had called for help? Reuven went into the kitchen again. There was another door a few steps up. He went through — and there, in the morning room, he saw the man in a wheel-chair. His head had fallen back, the Shofar and a Machzor had dropped onto the floor.

Quickly Reuven closed the door behind him, opened the window and went to the man. Unconscious, deathly pale . . . what did one do? There was artificial respiration . . . Then he remembered what he had heard of a new system: You hold the patient's nostrils closed and blow air into his lungs . . . You let the air come out again and repeat the procedure . . . He went to work on the patient.

Time passed; there was no change. Reuven was beginning to feel tired. He must get help. But he knew that artificial respiration must be continued without interruption, perhaps for hours . . .

What was he to do? Would all his work be in vain? He could not carry on much longer.

Then he heard steps, heavy steps, in the kitchen. The door opened — and a policeman, his truncheon raised, asked sternly: "What's going on here?"

Between breaths, Reuven explained: "Gas poisoning . . . artificial respiration . . . get help quickly . . ."

The policeman watched him for a moment. Then he said: "That's the idea . . . Keep it up and I'll be back in a tick."

Within minutes an ambulance arrived, and expert help took over. They found time, too, to bandage Reuven's leg.

When the family living in the house returned from Shul, Reuven learned the whole story. Mr. Leibowitz, who was half-paralysed, had insisted that they all go to Shul, and that he needed no attention and would even be able to blow Shofar for himself. He must have been in the middle of it when he smelt the gas, and being unable to reach the kitchen had done his best to attract attention by blowing the S.O.S. message on the Shofar.

As Mr. Leibowitz, now conscious, was carried into the ambulance, the family thanked Reuven and praised his courage and presence of mind, but he said: "it was *Min Hashomayim* that I should pass through your street at that precise moment."

SAFE SHELTER

REUVEN had been looking forward to this outing for a long time, and he really felt he needed one. He had been learning extra hard during Ellul, as had everyone in his Yeshivah. After getting up early for *Selichoth,* and what with Rosh Hashanah and Yom Kippur, followed by helping to put up the Succah both in the Yeshivah and at home, he had been quite exhausted by the time Succoth started. Now, after two days of Yom Tov he was ready for a day of fun and games in the forest.

He was going with the Pirchim group to which Shimon, his younger brother belonged, as nothing had been arranged for his own age group, and the Madrich was quite willing to have him as a sort of assistant.

However, when the group had assembled in front of the local railway station, the Madrich explained that because of rain in the past week he considered the forest too muddy; instead, he would take the group to the Science Museum, and afterwards, if it did not rain, to play football in Hyde Park.

Reuven was disgusted. He knew the Science Museum — or rather the children's section which would be all they would see — inside out, and had no intention of spending most of the day in there with a crowd of youngsters. It was a shame to drop the ramble at the last moment just because of a bit of mud. In a moment he had decided what to do.

He made an excuse to the Madrich, and so did Shimon, whom he had given a wink. When the group had boarded a bus and they were alone, he told Shimon of his plan. They

would go to the forest by themselves and have fun on their own. Shimon agreed, and they took the next train. For no reason at all a disturbing thought crossed Reuven's mind; was it quite right to go off to the forest without anyone knowing where they were? Supposing they were to have an accident... But he dismissed the idea. Why should anything go wrong?

The forest was indeed rather muddy and they had to make some detours where the path was flooded, but with the stout boots they were wearing, they were not much bothered by this and soon put a few miles between themselves and "civilisation", as they called built-up areas in the family idiom.

When lunch time came around Reuven trotted out an idea he had kept in reserve all along — to build a Succah in the forest. He had learned in the *Mishnah Berurah* that it was allowed to build a Succah on *chol-hamoed* even for one meal, and this was just the occasion to put it into practice.

Shimon was enthusiastic; they found a dry spot in a small clearing on high ground and collected a heap of dead branches. They marked out a space about four feet square, stuck strong sticks firmly into the ground and wove branches between them. Since they would sit on the ground, oriental fashion, they built only about four feet high, then laid branches across the top. To get a proper *S'chach* they heaped the roof with holly branches which still had their leaves on, some green, some dry but intact. To make the place warmer, they heaped branches and leaves against the walls outside. From afar the whole thing looked rather like a bush, but inside it was a cosy little place.

At the foot of the hill ran a stream and they dipped their hands in it before eating — for, as Reuven explained, this was as good as washing from a vessel. They sat in their Succah and ate their sandwiches, which tasted better than a proper meal at home.

After lunch Reuven brought out another of his ideas. Shimon was getting ready for his Barmitzvah, and knew most of his *Droshoh* by heart — but he still spoke too hurriedly and not loud enough.

Now Reuven practised on him what their father had done for him when he was learning his *Droshoh*. He made Shimon stand 20 paces away and say the first part of his *Droshoh*. For the next half hour he put him ruthlessly through the drill: "Stand up straight, but don't throw out your chest! Keep your chest full of breath! Don't throw your head back! Chin forward — imagine you are biting a piece of cake! Open your mouth and let the words roll out! Make your voice deeper! Louder, but don't shout! Slower, and clearer!

"Again: *'Moirai, — Veraboisai.'* '— When you say: *'Di Gemoroh zogt in Menochois Daf Mem'*, I must hear *'Di'* and *'in'* and *'daf'* just as clearly as the longer words!" And so it went on. Shimon begged for mercy, but Reuven explained that this was for his own good, to make him speak strongly and with confidence. They did not stop till Shimon had got the hang of it and began to enjoy it.

It was still too early to start back and they amused themselves in various ways: throwing the javelin with conveniently long sticks, high jumps over small bushes, finally climbing trees. And it was then that something did happen: jumping down from the last handhold, Shimon injured an ankle. It was only a sprain, but every step gave him great pain. Reuven helped him back into the Succah and took off his boots. The ankle was swollen, and although Reuven dipped their handkerchiefs in the stream and applied compresses it did not improve.

At home this would have been a minor matter — but how were they to get home? In his mind Reuven went over the route they had taken: jumping over boggy patches, thread-

ing their way through thickets — how was Shimon to manage all this even with his assistance? Leave him here and go for help? It would be dark before he was back, and how would Shimon feel all alone and unable to move?

Reuven now regretted the whole adventure bitterly. If the crowd had been here this would all be part of the fun, practising first aid and the transport of a "stretcher case", but alone . . .

But he must not let Shimon know his fears. "We'll easily get home," he told his brother. "We'll start in a few minutes. I'll find a stick for you, and you can lean on me. On the hard parts I'll carry you pick-a-back."

It was then they heard the car, bumping along a horse-track in low gear.

"Hurray! " exclaimed Reuven, "Here comes help. I'll run and stop them, and ask for a lift." But soon he had second thoughts. Something was wrong. Picnickers did not come into the forest so late on an autumn week-day, nor would they usually drive this far into the forest. He went back into the Succah.

"Let's wait," he said, "and stay inside quietly." The car came nearer and stopped at the stream. They heard people getting out. Two men were talking in low voices and coming nearer. They came in sight, passing not far from the Succah. They could see them through the foliage: two young men in flashy suits, leading between them a middle-aged man who seemed to be resisting and stumbled several times.

They disappeared into some bushes. After a few minutes the two young men came back alone.

"What have they done to the old man?" thought Reuven. "They must be kidnappers. Supposing they notice us! " But he calmed Shimon, who was shivering, and they kept quiet.

The men passed them and drove off the way they had

come. As soon as the boys were sure they had gone, they went in search of the third man, Shimon forgetting his pain in the excitement. They found him sitting against a tree trunk. He had been blindfolded and gagged, and tied hand and foot.

In a flash the boys had him free and were listening to his story. He was a Mr. Trevor, a bank manager. He had locked up the bank and got into his car as usual. When he was well out of town the robbers, who must have got into the car earlier with a duplicate key, and had been crouching low in the back, forced him at pistol point to drive into the forest. They had taken his keys and were only waiting for darkness to ransack the bank.

Without hesitation Reuven took charge of the situation. He made Shimon and Mr. Trevor comfortable in the Succah, then he pin-pointed the exact position on his map, and made his way as fast as possible to the nearest crossroads, where he knew there was a telephone.

From there he telephoned the police and gave all the details, including the address of the bank where the criminals could be trapped, and Mr. Trevor's home address, since he had asked for his wife to be informed. He also telephoned his parents, told them the whole story and assured them that Shimon was safe and that help was coming.

He had hardly finished when a police car arrived. Reuven got in and guided the driver through the forest. It was getting dark, but the car had a searchlight, and soon they had Shimon — his foot bandaged from the car's first aid kit — and Mr. Trevor safely in the car. Even before they got home they received a radio message that the criminals had been arrested.

Statements were taken from everyone concerned, and eventually Reuven had to give evidence in Court. When he described how they had observed the criminals without being seen by them, the judge interrupted to ask why they had built

the "hut" in the first place. He was interested in the idea of the Succah, and Reuven had to explain how it commemorated the huts built in the desert by the children of Israel, and the Divine protection they had received there.

The judge's comment was: "You certainly had Divine protection on this occasion. This hut probably saved your and Mr. Trevor's lives."

INSIDE THE LINE

GRAY AS THE DECEMBER SKY was Shaya's mood, as he stared out of the window of his bedroom, which he shared with a younger brother, over the untidy garden. He had run upstairs in a huff after a scene with his father.

It had not been a row — his father was a very learned Rabbi, a man of piety and reason — but all the same it was hard for Shaya. And it was all about a Menorah.

Most of Shaya's friends had shiny chromium-plated Menoroth and some had real silver-plated ones, but Shaya would still have to use the miserable tin affair he had had since he was a little boy! He, a boy of 14 and near the top of his class for Hebrew! He had begged his father for a new Menorah, but had been refused — oh so reasonably and patiently, but refused nevertheless.

"Look, Shaya", the Rabbi had said, "it isn't that I couldn't find the money. My salary isn't as grand as the money some of your friends' fathers earn, but I could find it if it were really necessary. But you have a Menorah. It is true that it is a great thing to make your Mitzvoth beautiful, but you have to be able to do it from your own money, without stinting anything important.

"If you want a Menorah, start saving from your pocket money and presents, till you can buy one from your own money."

"But that would take ages! " Shaya had objected.

"Ages? A year at the most, surely. Do you know that in all my Yeshiva years I lit Chanukah candles on a strip of tin?

Even after I married I had to borrow an old Menorah until Mummy decided to buy our silver one from money she had saved up. I even remember, in my home town, a very respected Baal Bos lighting, with olive oil and wicks, inside — you would never guess it — eight halves of potatoes scooped out to make oil lamps. I suppose he had had to pawn his Menorah and didn't manage to redeem it. Those were hard times..."

"Exactly, Daddy! Those were hard times, but nowadays people spend much more for all sorts of things. Surely we can do the same with a Mitzvah!"

"It is true," his father had said, "times are much easier — although not in all countries -- but the principle remains: people should spend what they can afford, after giving a good part for Tzedoko. I want you to learn this principle because most children nowadays are not learning it, and this might make them very unhappy when they get responsibilities of their own. I'll try to help you to save up. I'll give you — Bli Neder — a prize of 2/-for every Perek Mishnayoth you learn by heart; but you will have to pay for the Menorah, or at least for most of it, from your own money — and that's final."

What could you do if you had a father like this, Shaya reflected. It was no use arguing; and probably he was right too, so you couldn't even console yourself with the thought that you were suffering unjustly. It would take years and years till his wish was fulfilled.

Well, it was no use moping, and there was the garden to do. The children had shared out parts of the flower border to dig up and plant, as a kind of competition, and he, as the oldest, had chosen the hardest patch, a strip at the back which had to be cleared of rubbish thrown there in years past, before they had moved in, before it could be dug.

Shaya put on old togs and went out to the garden. He worked away solidly, gradually getting over his bad mood. He

started one heap for things to be burnt when they were dry enough, and another for iron scrap, broken tiles, pieces of a wash basin, and other useless stuff which he would put outside to be collected (with luck) by the dustman. Before long he started another small heap for salvage that could be sold to the ragman; a brass fender from a fireplace, a piece of lead pipe .... and then he found something that puzzled him : a flat piece of metal with a projection along one end and curious shapes cut on the other sides. The dark, greenish colour of the visible parts indicated brass; the shape was oddly familiar . . . He started scraping off the soil — surely this was a pair of lions, stylised as on Sefer Torah ornaments? What could it be? And what was this heavy projection at the bottom? Further scraping revealed hollow boat-shaped parts, eight of them . . . Of course! Nothing less than a Menorah, of a quaint antique design!

He had started to run to show it to his mother, when he stopped short. He must think this over. If his father heard of this he would not let him keep it, but start advertising for the owner or something. He hid the Menorah under his sweater and stealthily took it up to his room, where he left it on top of a cupboard.

Stealthily, too, he got rags and metal polish from the kitchen and started cleaning up the Menorah. Rag after rag was thrown away black, but at last the Menorah stood revealed in its full gleaming beauty, shining like gold, with hardly a black shadow where the engraving was deep. What a beauty! If only all went well, and nobody took it away from him . . .

All the rest of the day he thought of a way to find out the *din* about his find, and eventually hit on a plan. His class happened to be learning *Perek Eilu Metzioth*, and the next morning he asked his teacher:

"Suppose I find something valuable on a rubbish heap, where it has been for many years, could I keep it?"

"A good question, Shaya", answered the teacher, "we are really going to learn about it a few pages further. If a thing has definitely been thrown away, the finder can keep it. But if it is more likely to have been lost by some mistake like a fork or knife or a ring, which could have been thrown out with kitchen waste by mistake, then it is a lost article, which must be returned. If, as you say, it has certainly been there for years, we could assume that the owner has given up every hope of finding it, and it belongs to the finder. However, if by some chance the owner turns up, a good person ought still to give it back as a matter of *Lifnim mi-Shurath ha-Din,* going 'inside the line of the law'."

With that Shaya had to be content. Well, at least nobody could object to his keeping the Menorah. As for the owner turning up, surely that was not likely.

As he was going home with two of his friends that evening, they were discussing the teacher's answer. "Can you imagine", asked David Weiss, "anyone losing something on a rubbish heap? Surely if you lose something valuable you look everywhere for it, even in the dustbin?"

"I suppose it could happen," answered Osher Greenberg. "Something like that happened to my father. He had a beautiful old Menorah, which had been in the family for generations, and he lost it whilst he was in the Yeshivah. It happened like this: he fell ill and had to be in hospital for a long time. Whilst he was there, the hostel was moved to another house, and somebody packed up my father's things. When he came back from hospital, he couldn't find the Menorah. It must have been left behind where he had put it, wrapped up in brown paper at the back of a cupboard. He asked the people who had moved into the house, but they had not found anything; it may have been thrown away by the builders, together with waste paper and builder's rubbish — unless it was stolen."

Shaya didn't say anything, but he went home with a heavy heart. He happened to know that their house had been used as a Yeshivah-hostel during the war, and that Mr. Greenberg had been one of the students. It was more than likely that he had found the missing Menorah. But what was he to do? By law, the teacher had said, the Menorah was his. Mr. Greenberg had long given up hope, as Osher had told him. But then what about 'inside the line of the law'? Was he, Shaya, a "good" person, or was it good enough for him to keep to the strict law? This was not a question he could ask his father. He knew exactly what the answer would be: "You are a big boy, Shaya, and must give the answer yourself" — and at the same time he knew exactly what answer his father would expect. No, he had to make up his mind for himself before he said anything to his father.

How much he had looked forward to having at last a decent Menorah of his own, — and what a Menorah! Almost a work of art, certainly a beautiful piece of old-time craftmanship. Heaps better than a mass produced chromium thing . . .

But then, what about Mr. Greenberg? How happy would *he* be to have his family heirloom back after all these years, possibly the only thing to remind him of his family who had remained in Germany and never been found after the war!

With a deep sigh Shaya wrapped up the Menorah and without telling anybody at home anything, went straight to Mr. Greenberg. He found him in, and came straight to the point: "Mr. Greenberg, Osher told me you had once lost a Menorah. Could you tell me what it looked like?"

Mr. Greenberg was surprised at the question but, when

Shaya insisted that he *had* to know, gave him the exact description, even to the maker's initials on the back.

There was no doubt about it, it was the same Menorah; with some effort Shaya took it out of its wrappings and handed it to Mr. Greenberg, saying as calmly as he could: "Would it be this one?"

Before Mr. Greenberg could think of asking why and how, Shaya excused himself and ran out. He could not have contained himself any longer. But he knew he would always remember Mr. Greenberg's expression as he stood clasping the Menorah.

Next day during playtime, Osher came to him in great excitement and asked him how it had happened. Shaya told him the whole story, asking Osher not to tell anybody but his father, in confidence.

Came Chanukah. The family stood assembled waiting for father to begin lighting the candles. Shaya had prepared his old tin Menorah with its small candles. Suddenly, Shaya's father turned round and after a long look at Shaya said: "Well Shaya, are you happy now?"

"Yes Daddy," replied Shaya with a serious calm, "very happy." And he reflected how true this was; for every time he looked at the little tin Menorah he was reminded of the brass one, and although he felt a little sad about it, he also felt a great happiness at what he had done with it.

His father was still looking at him, and so were his mother and the children.

"Then," continued his father, "let's see how you'll feel when you have opened the parcel over there." And he pointed to the sideboard, where a paper parcel was lying.

In feverish haste Shaya tore off the wrapping, finding a brand new silver-plated Menorah fitted for oil or candles, the best any of his friends could show.

"Oh Daddy! " was all Shaya could bring out as he threw himself on his father and blubbered unashamedly.

"You see," the father explained, "Mr. Greenberg told me the whole story and insisted on giving me £ 1.— for you . . . so Mummy and I decided that since you had gone 'Lifnim mi-Shurath ha-Din,' it was up to us to do the same . . ."

DREAMS AND CHEESECAKE

He would never forget it . . .

It had been so beautiful . . . not just beautiful, there had been a kind of fear too, but so different from being afraid that fear was not really the word for it, and love, happiness, joy . . . oh, the joy! He had been sure he would not be able to bear the joy, he had thought he would die; perhaps he really had died . . . he felt quite different now from anything he had ever felt before, as if he were someone else . . . no, it was no use trying to give it words, but all the same he knew exactly what he had seen and heard. Never would he forget any of it.

But now he was tired, happy but tired . . . How good it was to lie back on the sheepskin couch; it was cool in the tent, miraculously cool. The cloud kept the summer sun away, and yet there was a refreshing breeze, a scented breeze . . . How good to rest in the shade.

How different it all was from the old life, only a few months ago: the heat, the dust, the hard, hard work even for the children, and the harsh orders, the threats and the beatings, and the fear that never stopped — sometimes it seemed as if it had been only a dream, a nightmare. But it was all gone now, it would never come back, of that he was sure, for they were quite different people now, Uri and his family and all the people; it could never happen to them again. It was curious that he should remember it now; he had tried hard to forget it these last months, and yet — now, after today, it somehow fitted into the picture, one could remember it now, and the bitterness itself was sweet to remember . . .

Yes, he would remember the bad time too, and how wonderfully it had all ended; how good Almighty God was to give them the new life...

Curious that after such a day one should think of food — and yet, it did not seem strange if one thought of it. Why should one not eat and be merry on a day like this, now that one had rested a little after the great things of the morning? And, he just remembered, no one had eaten all day; he had not even thought of it till now. What would there be for supper? Something festive surely. Roast lamb perhaps, like the day of freedom, or flavoured stew, or pot roast — he liked pot roast best of all... But why was there no smell of cooking? Where was his mother? Where was everybody?

With a shock Uri leapt up from the couch. Perhaps some further important things were going on and he had missed them! Hastily he washed his hands and face and put on his shoes and coat.

Outside the tent no one was to be seen. The stove was cold, the camp street deserted. No smoke, no cooking anywhere.

Then he heard voices from the day tent. Of course! The family must have assembled for supper — but what were they eating if there had been no cooking? He went into the tent. There were his parents, his brothers and sisters, all sitting round the white-covered table, dressed in their best garments — but on the table was only bread and milk; fresh milk, curds, cheese...

"How did you sleep, Uri?" his father greeted him smilingly. "We did not want to wake you, you seemed so tired. Come to the table and join in the feast." Uri returned the greeting and sat down. But he was puzzled — why was there no meat?

After a while he picked up the courage to ask his father:

"Why, on this great day, are we eating only milk food? Surely for such a festival we should kill a sheep?"

His father smiled: "I was waiting for you to ask this; now think and try if you can find the answer."

After a few moments, Uri suggested: "Perhaps there was no time to get everything done . . ."

"Not bad," said his father, "but we have pickled meat, and yet we eat cheese. Try again!"

Then Uri found it. "Of course! We are starting a new life; so many things have to be different . . . The slaughtering knife must be sharp and smooth, the tallow and some other parts must be removed . . ."

"And," completed his father, "it will take us some time to learn exactly how to do it all; and the pots can't be used until they are cleansed in boiling water; and still more things. So today we eat only milk food, and eat it cold; that is certain to be permitted; but it is not the meat that makes a feast — in the spirit of today, an ordinary meal is a feast!"

* * *

"You'd better have some cheesecake before it's all gone!" said Moshe, Uri's elder brother.

Uri rubbed his eyes. "Did I fall asleep?" He looked around; the Beth Midrash was brilliantly lit, the men and boys had closed their s'forim and were enjoying cake and coffee.

"Of course you slept, and soundly," scorned Moshe. "And how you begged to stay up! What about all the learning you planned to get done?"

"You think I learnt nothing?" countered Uri, "Why, I learnt . . ." But he decided not to tell everything just now; telling might spoil the beautiful memory. So he continued: "I bet you can't tell me the reason why we eat cheesecake on Shavuoth!"

STRANGE ENCOUNTER

IT WAS A foolish thing to do, of course, and I suppose I am lucky to be alive. One ought to listen to the advice of the inhabitants, especially in the wilder parts of Israel. All the same I don't regret the adventure.

I had been staying with my friend Moshe in Jerusalem, and since he had to visit Beer Sheva in connection with the new orthodox school — he works in the administration of that particular network — I seized the opportunity of a free ride to the Negev and came along. Moshe would be busy of course but he promised to ask a local man to show me the sights and generally take care of me.

However, when we arrived after a breakneck ride that started at dawn — all the drivers there are frustrated jet pilots and like nothing better than speeding on cliffside curves — it turned out that the local man was away for the day.

"Look here," said Moshe, "I'm terribly sorry, but I've got to attend to my affairs now; the school people are waiting. However, you are tired from the journey and soon it will get sizzling hot. I suggest you stroll around a little, anyone will show you the famous wells of Abraham. Then you go back to the hotel and have a good rest. Don't go out in the heat — please! It's the mistake all the tourists make. About three o'clock ask them to direct you to the Rabbi's house; you'll find him a very interesting man to talk to, and there I'll collect you when I'm ready. We'll still have an hour or two to do the sights before dark. And now, Shalom!" — And off he went.

Well, I was annoyed. Here I was with nothing to do for hours and hours, and in any case this midday rest business was not my cup of tea. All very well for these people who got up at a fantastic hour in the morning. They maybe could afford to knock-off at two o'clock for the day, or make a break from twelve to three. But I had paid for this; if I were to reckon only the fares my stay cost me five pounds a day. Why waste the best hours?

I soon got tired of sitting in the lounge. Suddenly I remembered that a friend from England was in a settlement near Beer Sheva, and when I asked where the place was I was told it was quite near — less than three kilometres and only half a kilometre from the road. It seemed one couldn't miss it. Just over half an hour's walk? Why, I could be there and back before Moshe was finished with his business!

Soon I was on the road. What nonsense all that fuss about the heat! Just nice and warm like a fine summer day in England. And yet so different: things looked brighter, distant things nearer and sharper — like an engraving rather than a painting. Both planted and wild parts had a strange, dreamlike, beauty. And there was no one to talk to for a change. I was free to make my own associations come to life. I could just imagine the patriarchs pasturing their sheep on these very hills, Abraham welcoming guests who had trudged along this age-old caravan road . . .

My mind was rather full of Abraham just then. The night before we had been talking about him quite a lot. Zahavah, Moshe's wife, was a teacher too (most young women of our circle were) and she had brought up the kind of questions the girls asked her. Very intelligent these Sabra children, I must admit, and their questions by no means easy to answer. We had been discussing this commentator and that, until I remarked: "I wish I could ask Abraham himself what really happened." And Moshe — he always makes bad jokes — had promptly rejoined: "Don't be in such a hurry, you'll meet him soon enough . . ."

All the same, I did wish Abraham was there. For one thing he could have given me a drink and some shade. It was getting a little hot, and the strong light was getting a little too much for me — I had not taken my sunglasses, I can't think why. And I was getting tired too. I must have walked an hour already and had not passed any settlement near enough to the road to be the one they had described.

In any case there were decidedly more turnings and branchings than the people in the hotel had mentioned. The trouble with me is that I speak Hebrew like a native, or anyway like a Meah Shearim man who has been to America; the immigrants round here aren't too hot in Hebrew themselves, so they take me for an Israeli. That I suppose, was why no one bothered to explain these little snags to me.

I wished I could stop somewhere and rest a little. But just then there was no shade in sight, no settlement or human being to be seen either. No, wait! There was something: believe it or not, a Bedouin encampment! I could distinctly see the black tents, and quite a lot of them too, not half a mile down the road, a little to the left of the road — and sheep, lots of them, all over the hillside, lying down most of them, ruminating I suppose. Well, I would go to the camp and sample their famous hospitality. They were bound to be friendly so near the town and in broad daylight.

I quickened my step — or rather I tried to — my feet didn't quite respond. The heat was getting me after all. Lucky I had come to this place in time. They seemed to have spotted me too. There was a lad running towards me, about fourteen maybe. Very Jewish-looking he was, if you know what I mean, and with nothing like the "I-don't-know-you" bearing of the Arabs I had seen in the towns. Perhaps they got like that when they grew up. He wasn't dressed in the white shirt and headcloth of those Arabs either. In fact I had never seen such a kind of dress before, except on some picture in an archaeology book — Egypt, was it? Yes, probably Egypt by the shape of that picture: a long line of people, men, women and children, all dressed more or less alike in a clinging long garment, white with spots or flowers in a regular pattern. That was what the boy was wearing, except that he had a huge headcloth draped over his arms as well, rather like a tallith ... So many different kinds of people in Israel nowadays, I thought; you don't know whom you'll meet next.

He had come up to me and made a very deep bow, all in one sweeping movement, very oriental and quaint. And then he spoke. It sounded very Arabic, full of gutturals, but I soon realised he was speaking Hebrew. Not modern Hebrew either, by the style of it; rather a classical Hebrew, biblical I should call it, although he used a number of words that were definitely not in the Bible and that I had to guess at rather than understand.

And then I remembered what it said under that picture: "Semites bringing tribute". It may have been the heat of course, but I tell you from that moment on I was not really surprised at anything that followed.

What the boy was saying in a rather long-winded and embellished way was to the effect that I, his lord and master, would honour and delight his grandfather — the Haham or whatever I should call him — if I would have the goodness to step into his tent and accept whatever little thing he could put before me. His grandfather was very old apparently, and was quite heartbroken at not being able to come out and welcome me as was fitting.

What did I tell you? Oriental hospitality at its classical best.

I did my best to reply in style, and went along with the boy. Or to tell the truth, I went very much leaning on him, for he had noticed the shape I was in and insisted on supporting me. But I reached the big tent eventually — quite a pavilion, raised up on poles so that one had a view of the countryside in every direction. And there was the leader, a majestic but friendly white-bearded man, dressed in gold-embroidered damask, getting up from his ivory-studded couch just as I came in and bowing to me before I could get my own greeting in. Greetings completed, he made me comfortable on a couch that felt like foam-rubber but actually was built up from layers of sheepskin rugs. Drinks were brought — I found the chilled buttermilk best, which was served from a jug kept inside one of those huge water-jars of porous clay — and when they saw that I still did not feel comfortable they brought me a wet headcloth and led me to a smaller tent to rest a while.

Soon I felt as fit as a fiddle; the boy took me to an ablution tent to "wash my feet". I used the opportunity to wash throughly with the water the boy poured for me. Then we went back to the reception tent, and I was left alone with my host whilst we waited for the meal to be served — for he had begged me to stay, if not for the night, at least for a meal and until the heat went down, and I had accepted gratefully. I had forgotten all about my appointment with Moshe. In fact, I had forgotten everything except the wonder of the old man's smile and the extraordinary quality of his conversation.

At first I was tongue-tied — a very unusual condition for me; I was frankly over-awed by the splendour of my host's presence. The radiant friendliness of his smile was something

I had never before experienced; and when he turned his eyes full upon me — well, I am not normally addicted to deep emotional experiences; quite the reverse, in fact; but those eyes — they somehow suffused my whole being in one great glow of kindliness and love. I remember thinking to myself: "This is what it must be like to look into the eyes of an angel — or a patriarch . . ."

But very soon the boy brought wine, in primitive-looking leather flasks, and after the first few sips I began to feel more at ease. It was good wine, exceptionally good, in fact, in spite of the slight tang of the leather which clung to it, and I began to enter more into the conversation, which up to now had been slightly one-sided. My host, whose name I could not quite catch — Ibraheem something-or-other, it sounded like — led me on to speak about what interested me most at the moment. This was the problem of Abraham I had been thinking about. Probably due to the influence of local colour it had been in the forefront of my mind since that morning. Seeing that my host was obviously the distinguished Haham of a nomadic Jewish community at the very least, I decided to broach the problem to him. You never know, he might have an original view-point to put forward; these primitive types very often had.

What I got was something utterly unexpected; something that even today I can neither properly explain — nor forget . . .

I put forward my problem. I could not understand why our forefather Abraham, who risked his life against impossible odds to rescue his nephew Lot from the clutches of the Four Kings, nevertheless refused to raise a finger to protect his own wife when she was taken prisoner first by Pharaoh and then again by Abimelech.

My host's reaction to this innocent question shocked and amazed me. Those eyes were again turned full upon me, but this time when, as if drawn by an invisible force, I looked into their depths, I saw a flame of pure anger burning there — a flame which seemed to penetrate to the core of my being and burn up all the littleness inside me.

My host spoke. His voice came to me as if from a great distance, but I could not mistake the vibrant intensity of his reply.

"Fight Pharaoh?" said the voice. "Die fighting for *my right*? for *my honour*?" The ironic intonation was intense. "That might count as a noble thing with the Philistines or other sea-peoples, but in the way of God one does not die for pride or for honour. One prays, one suffers, if need be, accepting the justice of God, but one survives. There are better things to use one's life for than as a monument to one's own glory.

"But Lot?" went on that voice, riveting me to the spot, paralysed, but with my heart wildly beating. "Lot? — I bring heaven and earth to witness that this was for no other glory than for the glory of God! To lay down one's life for justice and for right — what could be a better end than this?"

In my disturbance of mind I must have got up and walked out of the tent, for the next thing I knew a piercing light was hurting my eyes, and through the light came half-a-dozen figures carrying rifles. "There he is!" exclaimed a voice.

Then they were standing around me and the one with the red Magen-David on his arm was feeling my pulse. "What's the matter?" I asked in a confused way, "Can't you leave a man alone?"

I had spoken in English and it was Moshe who answered, "Take it easy, old man, we'll soon have you right. You've had sunstroke, but since you've survived till now you'll be alright. What on earth possessed you to go and camp in the open?"

"In the open?" I protested. "Why, I've been under canvas all the time, and a jolly good time they gave me, I can tell you."

"Under canvas?" wondered Moshe. "You mean those Bedouins down the road? But they've sworn they hadn't seen anything of you, and they haven't, I'm sure. They wouldn't have let you out again in your condition; it's against their principles. You can't imagine what a time I had when you were missing. The frontier police here have been driving round for hours until we spotted you."

And so it went on. According to Moshe I had collapsed by the roadside and dreamt the rest, and so thought the others. My only ally was the doctor, and all he would commit himself to was that if I had had sunstroke I had by now recovered from it completely, for he could not find a single symptom. And indeed I reached the jeep under my own steam and feeling perfectly fit, though I was grateful for the blanket they gave me, for the night was cold.

When I got back to my hotel room and the familiar electric light and h & c, I was almost ready to come round to their way of thinking. The whole episode began to seem most unreal, and I was hard put to explain it even to myself. It would certainly be more comfortable to write it all off as a touch of sunstroke and try to forget all about it — if possible . . .

However, sitting on the bed, I discovered that I was still clutching something. I looked at it. It was a leather wine-flask of very peculiar make. I have since taken it to an archaeologist friend of mine. He seemed very excited when I showed it to him, and said it seemed to be of a kind in use in Canaan in the second millenium B.C.E. — in fact, in the time of Abraham. He is trying to persuade me to let him send it away for the radio-activity dating test, and is furious with me for not being able to tell him clearly how I got hold of it. Frankly, I am not at all sure myself what to make of it all.

TEST CASE

I WISH I HAD resigned right at the start of the affair. What's the good of being Minister of Labour if no one listens to you? It is hard enough to handle legitimate priests once they go in for Politics, but this pair of visionaries . . . I just can't fathom their mentality.

Come to think of it, I can't understand anything about them — from the moment they walked into the Audience Room. The guards later swore they had not come past them. It is a pity we did not believe them — just now we could do with extra men, and probably they told the truth after all. There was a stable boy who claimed to have seen them come in from the lions' enclosure, but at the time it seemed impossible, so he was condemned too, poor fellow.

However they got in, there they were: two ageing men in tribal dress addressing the King about this wild idea of a pilgrimage into the desert, of all places, to meet a god never heard of before.

Everything went wrong from the start. I mean to say, we all know that His Majesty's wisdom is divine, but what is the point in having ministers if you act without consulting them? He should never have sent those two away with a commonsense answer — should never have sent them away at all. Anyone could see they were dangerous — particularly the one with the stammer. He can't open his mouth, lets the other speak for him — and suddenly he looks at you . . . and you feel every single sane and rational idea you have ever had tottering under his challenge. That first minute I said to myself: he is not natural, that one, he is in league with some spirit, we will not have a moment's peace as long as he is alive.

But no, His Majesty chooses that very moment to assert himself as a diplomat. Well, I suppose he felt the same challenge and just had to react to it in his own royal way. But I could have told him even then that he was handling it wrongly. You can't meet that kind of thing with rational arguments.

And you can't cure that kind of labour trouble with disciplinary measures. How long it took to build up that system of collective responsibility, getting the very solidarity of these tribesmen to work in our favour! The Workers' Council was the most wonderful instrument ever invented. With them he should have reasoned — after getting rid of the ringleaders. But no, to them, our only real contacts with the masses, he talks of punitive work — and has them flogged when they can't get it done. He got his increased production in the end, but what good was that! A child could have told him that his methods merely united the workers against us and, instead of stifling the rebellion, fanned it into flame.

When you get a King joining battle with a visionary, and with the labour force too — why, then you can just say good-bye to diplomacy and wise counsel and wait for the worst.

And the worst came, step by inevitable step — though I must say I did not expect it to come in just that way. Ten months, by all that's holy! Blood in your water-pitcher, frogs in your dinner plates — and lice! He made us look ridiculous all right, that man with the strange ideas. And he made out his case all right: a deity who can send hailstorms on a land that does not know rain, and cattle plagues and skin diseases, and take them away again, all on the predicted hour — He exists all right, and is worth obeying.

We ought to have cut our losses long ago; there is not one man in the kingdom who does not say so. Let them go, let them perish in their precious desert if they insist! We'll be left a poor country, we'll have to call-up our own people for labour, but at least we'll live.

That is what everybody says — except His Majesty. Oh, not always, to be sure; when each disaster has struck he is reasonable enough — but only for a few days. Then he must again make a stand, for civilization, for reason, for the gods. He makes a brave stand; history will praise his superhuman courage — but as for me, whenever I hear him declare his defiance I shudder. It is not natural. This may be a blasphemous thought, but it seems to me that in his own way he is just as much a tool of the strange deity as is that man Moses.

And not he alone, worse luck. We have dealt with mad kings before; nothing is easier than to arrange some accident if public opinion is ripe. But His Majesty is not mad, or if he is then we are too — each time he makes his brave and noble speech we all rally.

But where will it end? It has long stopped being Politics and become a battle of ideas. Tonight it will become a battle of gods. The new Deity, having proved His power over nature, has announced that tonight He will destroy the gods — and that one person in each house will die without being ill.

Surely that is going too far! Surely He cannot make that happen — unless He is indeed supreme over men and gods, Master of death and life!

Soon we shall know.

I am glad my scribe can write in this unnatural darkness — it is just possible I shan't have another chance to record this.

I happen to be a firstborn son myself.

THE KING'S MEN

A LONG TIME AGO in the time of King Solomon there was a boy named Shama who grew up on a small island in the Red Sea. His father was stationed there to signal the approach of ships to the distant mainland by flashing mirrors in the day and by fires at night. Shama had not been to the mainland since he was small. He did not know any people apart from his parents and the few sailors who brought their supplies.

But the time came when a relief arrived and the family were taken to Eylath.

There Shama saw many new things. There were sailors and fishermen, porters and shipbuilders all working very hard in the hot sun, whilst other men in clean clothes did nothing but supervise them.

The same day his father took him along to the splendid residence of the Governor, to whom he had to make a report, and Shama wondered why the King gave power and riches to some men and hard work to others.

The next day the family set out for Jerusalem, where the father had to report at Court. Just before they came to the Dead Sea where they were to board another boat, they met a gang of many men who were chained together and forced to drag huge blocks of stone. His father told him that these were the King's prisoners, building a new fortress, and Shama was frightened of a King who punished people so hard and wished they did not have to go to his Court — who knew what might happen to them if he got angry!

But when they had arrived in Jerusalem his father insisted that he must come along, saying, "This might be your only chance of ever seeing the inside of the Palace." So Shama was washed and anointed and dressed in his best, and was even allowed to go with his father to the Public Audience in the throne room where everything glittered with gold and rare stones. But when the King had entered he noticed the boy and when he had found out who he was commanded that he come before him.

Shama was trembling when he was being led to the foot of the steps flanked by gold lions, but Solomon spoke to him kindly: "My son, you have just seen our country for the first time, and I want you to tell me what was the strangest thing of all you have seen." When Shama hesitated he continued, "Nay, do not fear! Tell me truly, for he who wishes to be wise must hear everyone."

Shama mustered all his courage and said: "Your Majesty, I have seen many of your servants. Why do some of them live in palaces and others have to work so hard on the ships — and others still wear chains and do very hard labour in the desert? Would it not be more just to treat them all alike?"

Solomon smiled at the boy and answered: "You are right and brave to ask what puzzles you, for only by asking can you learn. All the men you saw are working for me whilst I myself am only another overseer, for we all work for God and for each other. But I and my Ministers have to give each man the work he can do best. The shipwright would not be able to be a Governor and the Governor would do a poor job on a ship. We also have to give each man what he needs and the Governor must have a palace so that the people and he himself should realise his importance and responsibility. As for the prisoners, they are men who disobeyed orders and have to learn and show the others that they cannot avoid serving their King and their people. Do you understand it now, or is there anything you want to ask?"

Seeing the King so kind Shama asked: "And why did my parents have to spend all these years on a rocky island, and I also, when others can live at home? Have we done anything wrong to deserve this?"

"Your father," replied the King, "is a brave and loyal man who has done a hard and important task willingly and well. Now he goes home to the farm his brother has been looking after and takes with him this purse of gold to reward his long and loyal service. But you who ask so cleverly and bravely shall stay in Jerusalem and receive all the teaching you have missed. In five years we shall see what task can be entrusted to you."

* *
*

Like Shama we come into this world and see many strange and frightening things. We see some people ill and others well; some rich and others poor, and we get frightened about what may happen to us.

But on Rosh Hashanah we come before the King of kings and learn that these things come not by accident but by His judgment. On Rosh Hashanah God assigns each of us his special task that cannot be done by anyone else, whether it be one of power and responsibility like the Governor's, or the hard and lonely work of Shama's father, or just the daily labour of ordinary men — we only pray that we shall not be like the prisoners who do the King's work against their will. But God is merciful as well as just and if we ask Him He will help us to find our faults and to remove them, and when we really try to do better He forgives our past sins and helps us to carry out the task He sets us.

And when, like the boy in our story, we want to know

more about Him and the way He wishes His world to be, He helps us to understand His Torah — and perhaps will give us a specially responsible position amongst those who do His work.

APPENDIX

The Prisoner

The story is collected from traditional sources. Abraham's thoughts on sun and moon come from *Sefer Hayashar* (Seder Hadoroth 1958) the idol-breaking and the discussion between Abram (as he was then called) and Nimrod from *Bereshith Rabbah,* 39,19.

The death of Abram's brother Haran (*Targum Y. Ber.* 11, 28 and *Rabba,* end of Noah, have different versions) has been omitted. It is important in that it contradicts our assumptions on two points: a) if Haran, who had children, died as a result of the occurences of our story, then Abraham would have been older than I made him, (but cf. *Sanh.* 69b), and b) if Haran died at Nimrod's hands (*Rabba* but not *T.Y.*), the ending is not as happy as I made it. — In any case, the age at which Abraham recognised God is disputed (Rabba Vayigash 95,2), being 3 or 48. Rambam, (*Mishneh Torah, Hilchoth Avodath Kochavim, ch.* I, from where the theology of the priest in our story has been taken) reads 40 (see commentaries) but speaks of an earlier gradual recognition; *Kessef Mishnah* (ibid.) and *Yuchasin* reconcile the two opinions in the Midrash in this sense.

The concealment of Abraham as a child is taken from *Sefer Hayashar* (as quoted by *Seder Hadoroth* 1948), though the place of concealment is there deşcribed as a cave, where Abraham and his nurse spend 10 years, after which (*S. HD.* 1958) he spends another 39 years with Noah and Shem. This too argues for putting Abraham's preaching later. Also, in the Talmud (*Ab. Z.* 9a) his age is given as 52 when (starting on?) making converts at Ḥaran (which may be the extant town of Harran 37° N. 39° E.).

The weight of the evidence is, then, in favour of making Abraham a grown man at the time of our episode.

The chief point in favour of telling the story about a *young* Abraham is perhaps that I remember it so from *Cheder,* and assume that children prefer to imagine it this way.

Abraham's birthplace is given by Bachya (S.HD. 1948) as Kutha, which in *Bab. Bath.* 91a occurs as one of the places of his imprisonment (by his father or Nimrod) and is there identified with Ur Kasdim. I have assumed as the place of his birth and of our story the town excavated at Tel el Muqayyar (about 200 km S.E. of Babylon) in 1922-9 by Sir Leonard Wooley and described in "Ur of the Chaldees". He found buildings and objects which exhibit a high degree of craftsmanship and artistry. Houses dated at the time of Abraham had up to 14 rooms on two floors, with an underground drainage system. Vaulted cellars served as family graves. Clay tablets recorded business accounts, law cases, mathematics (up to cube roots) and poetry.

As model for Nimrod, I have taken Sargon of Akkad who, like other northern kings after him, made his daughter high-priestess to Nannar the moon god at Ur, although the date assigned to Sargon by Wooley (2630 BCE) is too early for our dating of Abraham. The description of the palace with its hunting pictures comes from an excavation in Assyria.

The story is intended chiefly to convey the revolution of thought started by Abraham. If in the process I have made the king too liberal and his priests too wise, I plead the necessity for a framework for the discussion which is the heart of the story.

We Attack at Midnight

The story is based on *Bereshith* 14, with full use of *Yalkut Shimoni.* I have tried to reconcile the opinions there as to the part played by Eliezer.

That Abraham's address included points prescribed in the Torah (*Dev.* 20) is mentioned in *Yalkut;* we would also expect it from the fact that "Abraham kept the Torah before it was given" (*Yoma* 28b). His motive for the fight is in part taken from *ReDak* and *Sforno,* and in part my conjecture, as is his offer of freedom in case of failure, and the "children coming to learn" (which is meant to represent the *kiddush Hashem* — by analogy with King David's proselytes in Yebamoth 79a).

The stratagem of nocturnal surprise (as in Judges 7) is taken from *Sforno* and *ReDak.* The miraculous harmlessness of the enemy weapons is one of two interpretations of *Yeshayah* 41,2 quoted in *Yalkut* here.

The Boy in the Basket

The facts come from *Shemoth,* 2 and *Yalkut,* where dates, ages etc. are mentioned. Thus the date 6th Sivan (Shevuoth) results from

Mosheh being 3 months old; he was born 7th Adar (and died on the same date). Another opinion there makes it 21st Nisan (the date of *kriath yam suf*) by assuming an Adar Sheni and incomplete 3 months. Exceptional heat led Bitiah to bathe — her cure from a skin disease at the moment of finding Mosheh swayed her to overrule the objections.

I have made Miryam a kind of assistant nurse. According to the opinion (*Sota* 11b) which is the source for it, she was a midwife together with her mother. I have met a midwife, now retired, who went out to births with her grandmother when aged 16, in England.

I have assumed the location to be near Thebes, as this was, according to historians, the capital city from 2100-1100 B.C.E. (the exodus was 2448 A.M., 1312-B.C.E.), so as to make it possible for Bitiah to bathe near the Hebrew village. This required treating the village as a colony separated from the main Hebrew settlement, which seems to have been at the eastern extremity of the Nile delta — for Pitom and Raamses are identified by *T.Y.* (*Shemoth* 1,11) as Tanis and Pelusium (now ruins near Port Said), as are the original settling in "the land of Raamses" (*Ber.* 47.11) and the Raamses from which the exodus started out (*Shemoth* 12,37).

However it may well have been the other way — that Pharaoh had a second residence in the Delta, where Memphis had, in an earlier period, been the capital.

The name Toviah as the name his mother gave him comes from *Yalkut*. Bitiah's remark on an Egyptian meaning for "Mosheh" is meant to account for the fact that this name, for which the Torah gives a Hebrew derivation, is also found as part of Egyptian names.

He Went Home

The main facts come from *Shemoth*, 2, and *Yalkut*. The slave's story about the start of the oppression may be found in greater detail in *Seder HaDoroth* (2340). The crime of the overseer is described in *Yalkut* (166, end and 167, end), and my description of the killing is an attempt to reconcile the opinions in the latter passage.

My rendering of Mosheh's flight, however, departs from tradition; according to *Yalkut* (167) he was arrested and condemned to death, and only escaped "the sword of Pharaoh" by a miracle.

Moshe's meeting with his family is conjecture, based on such slender clues as that he recognised the voice of his father (*Yalkut* 171) and apparently knew his brother (*Shemoth* 4,14). However, from *Yalkut* (166) it appears that such a meeting took place before he went out to his brethren.

The age of Mosheh as 18 is one opinion in *Yalkut;* another gives it as 20.

The name Uri is invented. Uri, father of Bezalel, was not yet born, acording to Sanh. 69b.

For Thebes as the capital, see notes to "The Boy in the Basket." The description of the chariot comes from archaeology.

The Torah tells us little about the 60 years intervening between our episode and Mosheh's return — according to *Yalkut* (167) all this time was spent in Midian, according to another tradition (*Yalkut* 168) most of it in Kush. — It would seem that the Torah tells nothing which is of merely historical interest; what it does tell is sufficient to sketch Mosheh's character as a lover of Israel and of justice.

The final speech of Amram in the story is meant to suggest a reason for this long maturing period. We learn (*Yalkut* 169,3) that "Mosheh was tested with sheep" (for patience and mercy).

Three Hundred Men

The story is a plain rendering of Judges 6-8, without any "dramatization". The rise of the dialogue from the words of a prophet who turns out to be an angel to Gideon's own prophecy is described in Scripture itself, and explained in *Yalkut*: Gideon had earned a right to hear the voice of God by defending Israel, and that is the "strength" mentioned in the prophecy: strong is he who believes in a mighty cause.

The return to God seemed to me the essence of the story, and the victory a necessary consequence; that is why I did not try to dramatize the latter, and left out details of the pursuit.

The first paragraphs of the story are meant to explain why Gideon, whom we find giving orders to 10 servants, was threshing the wheat alone. Yether is mentioned (8,20) as a young boy, though I have perhaps assumed him too young.

Matzoth (see Judges 6,19) come into our story not only because they can be baked quickly, but also because the time was Pesach (*Yalkut*). Wheat must have been unripe indeed at the start of barley harvest, that is why I assume that the barley had been destroyed.

The capture of Gideon's brothers, and the punishment of the enemy chiefs for murdering them, are mentioned Judges 8, 18-21.

The year, according to *Seder HaDoroth,* is 2676 A.M. (1084 B.C.E.).

The Girl from Moab

The story follows the book of Ruth; *Yalkut Shimoni* was consulted. Non-Jewish writers have treated this as a love story, by straining the facts considerably. Bo'az describes himself as not being a young man. According to tradition he was old indeed and a widower, and died soon after marrying Ruth. The marriage, and the birth of Oved, are indeed the culmination of the story, but the central problems are clearly those attending Ruth's way into Judaism and Jewry.

The girl Naarah in my version is invented (after the captive in II Kings, 5) to introduce Jewish ideas as seen by Ruth in her childhood. The name Ruth is interpreted (*Yalkut*), from the root *"rathoth"*, to tremble, as "she who fears sin", i.e. her moral sense was exceptional. She was (*Yalkut*) a granddaughter (Others: daughter) of king Eglon who had shown respect for God (Judges 3,20), a descendant of Balak who had sacrified to God (*Bamidbar*, 23). These trends crystallised in Ruth; to make Ruth possible, her whole nation was spared by divine command (*Bab. K.* 38b).

The sons of Elimelech had married Ruth and Orpah without their having become proselytes; they were not even aware (*Yalkut*) that the prohibition against marrying Moabite proselytes does not apply to females. Even in the time of Saul this ruling still found opponents, and the *Beth Din* of Samuel had to be invoked to confirm it (*Yeb.* 77a).

The Beginning

(See also notes to "No Sleep That Night").

The story aims to describe the moral and historic background to the Purim story — it belongs more to Ta'anith Ester than to Purim.

The period falls in between the revocation of the permission to build the temple (Ezra 4, 11-24) and the new permission (Ezra 6). All calculations of the "70 years of Babel" (Jer. 29,10) had been proved wrong. Achashverosh himself had expected the prophecy to be fulfilled in the 2nd year of his reign, and it was the fact that nothing developed then which emboldened him to use the holy vessels at the festivities in his 3rd year (*Meg.* 11b). It was seen only after the event that the prophecy was fulfilled in two parts: 70 years after the exile of Yechonyah Jews returned to the Holy land, and 70 years after the destruction of the temple it was finally rebuilt, but the two stages of both exile and redemption were separated by 18 years. During those 18 years, faith was under strain.

Assimilation and laxness in mitzvoth had made inroads. We find Ezra and Nechemyah dealing with mixed marriages (Ezra 9 and 10) and desecration of the Shabbath (Neh. 10,32). Our sages (*Meg.* 12a) trace the sin that caused the decree of Haman back to honouring the statue erected by Nebuchadnetzar (Dan. 3), but since the sins of the fathers are visited upon their children only if these continue the sin (Sanh. 27b) we have to find a continuing fault, and this seems to lie in a general tendency to surrender Jewish ideals and laws under outside pressure. Eating at the king's party, though rejected as the cause in *Meg*. 12a, because the Jews outside Shushan had no part in it, is mentioned in *Midrash Esther* (7, "*R. Yishmael*") as the cause.

The character of Shaltiel is invented.

This story was written later, and for an older age-group, than "No Sleep That Night," and departs from it in some of the minor facts assumed, but is similar in aim.

If the two stories are read together, they will lose in impact.

No Sleep That Night

This story is a different (earlier) treatment of Purim from "The Beginning"; it is meant for a younger age-group and tells more of the actual story of Purim.

It is often not realised that the crisis of the Purim story took place just before and on Pesach; here the connection is stressed. I have followed *Yalkut* by describing the fasts as being broken each evening, so that *Seder* was kept, although in the Talmud (*Yeb*. 121b) it would appear that they went on for the whole three days without interruption.

Facts not found in Scripture come from *Yalkut*.

The Recruit

The Chanukkah story is too often seen as a military feat rather than the victory of spirit it represents. As an attempt to rectify this, this version tells very little of the actual story but concentrates on the problem of one of the contemporaries it affected. It has in the process perhaps become too wordy.

Start of a War

A rendering of the story in the Talmud (*Gittin*, 55b), expanded but not dramatized. Josephus, *Jewish War*, was drawn upon for some political data.

The Long Net

Based on the narrative in the Talmud (*Pesachim* 3b), the story has been expanded to describe procedure of the Sanhedrin, the appearance of the *Beth Hamikdash* (taken from *Middoth, Bab. Bath*. 4a, and other sources), and the *Korban Pesach* (*Mishnah Pes*. 5,5-7).

R. Yehudah's town would seem to be the extant Nsibin (41° E., 37° N.). His time is difficult to establish. We find a *tanna* of this name with R. Yoshua and R. Eliezer (*Ed*. 8,3; *Neg*. 9,3 and 11,7); if this is our R.J.b.B., he would belong to the generation surviving the destruction, and the *Nasi* of his time would probably be R. Shimon b. Gamliel I, who succeded his father 18 years before the destruction.

In that time, the Sanhedrin no longer dealt with capital crimes as a rule. The desecrator in our story was eventually killed (*Pes.* 3b), but as a gentile he might not have been affected by ordinary practice; in fact, he might fall in any case into that class of desecrators which was not dealt with by the Sanhedrin but by the priests (Sanh. 81b).

When first writing the story, I had assumed an earlier date for R. Jehudah b. B. since Maimonides (Preface to Mishnah commentary, ch. 4) apparently puts him very early, and assumed the *Nasi* of his time to be R. Gamliel I. I have now deleted all names and references which would commit us to a definite period, so that at the expence of weakening the style a little I have avoided controversy.

The name of the gentile is invented, and his town Arbela (which I assume to be Erbil, 44^0 E., 36^0 N.) was chosen arbitrarily as a likely town from which travellers would pass through Nsibin.

My Cow Broke a Leg

The story of how R. Eliezer came to learn Torah is told in *Avoth de-Rabbi Nathan* VI/3, *Ber. Rabbah* 42/1 and *Pirkei de-Rabbi Eliezer* 1-2. The versions vary on details: his age at the time is given as 22 in *A.dR.N.* and 28 in *P.dR.E.;* in *A.dR.N.* it appears that he was married or betrothed, whilst in *P.dR.E* his father tells him to get married and in time send his children to study rather than try to become a scholar himself. I have tried to avoid points in which the sources contradict; on the other hand I have introduced details which seemed to be implied in the traditional story, and have invented some others. For instance, the sources give us no information on the location of the farm, beyond implying that it was on a hillside. We do know that later Rabbi Eliezer resided at Lod (*Sanh.* 32b) and that when he died he was carried from Caesaria to Lod for burial (*Sanh.* 68a), and I have assumed for the purpose of the story that the family came from that district; the name "Kfar Zecharyah" is inspired by an Arab village a few miles east of Lod, but is not meant to be exact.

The central problem of the story — sacrificing material security for Torah study — recurs in every generation, and every Yeshivah has some unsung heroes who, in their way, followed R. Eliezer's example.

They Called Him a Traitor

A rendering of the story in the Talmud (*Gittin* 56a).

A Pearl of Great Price

A rendering of a tale published by S.A. Wertheimer in "Batei Midrashoth" (new edition Jerusalem 5712/1952) from a Yemenite manuscript. Its title is "Maasseh Rav Kahana ve-Selik Bno". The tale is undoubtedly very old, though its exact age is difficult to establish. My tentative opinion is to place it around 1000 C.E., on the strength of the fact that it uses names of *Amoraim* together with names known only from the time of the *Gaonim*. If we take the story to be fiction, the story-teller might have chosen at random names still famous in his time without attempting to commit himself to a definite period.

The original has a beauty of its own which neither re-telling nor translating can reproduce completely. I have left out the discussion of the halachic problem, since any halachic value it might have is best left to the experts, and have treated it as merely a tale with a moral.

He Sleeps and Slumbers Not

A rendering of a story in "Ungekanntes Judentum" by Judaeus, going back to a tradition which I believe I have heard told independently of that book.

The Tenth Jew

The chief facts in the story are a chassidic tradition which has been printed in Hebrew before. Details, such as the remark on "the 50th year", are my elaboration — I can only hope that it does not do the Rabbi an injustice.

The Price of an Ethrog

Adapted from a story told by Judaeus in "Ungekanntes Judentum" as factual. The discussion on *bittachon* etc. is my addition.

Ghostly Clock

The Rabbi in the story was my teacher. The story is factual, but the reflections contained in it are my additions.

Buried Treasure

The story is, of course, fiction, but fiction has its own rules: it must be possible and momentarily believable. Britain at the time of the destruction of the temple had been a Roman possession for over 100 years (though I have not checked up on Cornwall); the tin mines were older still. Jews exiled to Britain are mentioned by the Sages. The *tannaim* kept private notes of versions of the Mishnah.

Note for American readers: "Yeshivah" in these stories has the European meaning of a place of full time Hebrew instruction which boys join after leaving school.

S . . . O . . . S . . .

The story is pure fiction.

Safe Shelter

The story is fiction, and no reference to any real person is intended. The *dinim* mentioned have been checked up.

Inside the Line

The story is based on a real case, though not told exactly as it happened. The *dinim* are correct in my opinion.

Dreams and Cheesecake

Various reasons are given for the *minhag* to eat dairy food on Shavuoth; the one assumed here is given in *Mishnah Berurah* 494,12. I have never dared to describe *Mattan Torah* in a story, and this sketch of how a child might have reacted to it is the nearest approach to it I found possible.

Strange Encounter

First published in "Yeshurun", Dec. '56.

The story is pure fiction. I have never been to Be'er Sheva and cannot even vouch for the geography. It originated as a vehicle for the explanation of Abraham's actions.

Mr. Aryeh Carmell kindly revised the story for me. From the paragraph beginning: "My host's reaction" onwards it is mainly his wording, and the "leather flask" is his idea.

Test Case

First published in "Yeshurun", Spring '57.

This is, of course, not an ancient papyrus, but a vehicle for the *midrash* and own explanations contained in it.

The King's Men

The story is fiction, invented to serve as a parable for the thoughts expressed at the end.